The Bobbsey Twins at the County Fair

The Bobbsey Twins at the County Fair

by Laura Lee Hope

Wilder Publications, LLC.
PO Box 3005
Radford VA 24143-3005

ISBN 10: 1-61720-303-3
ISBN 13: 978-1-61720-303-9

Table of Contents:

The Broken Bridge

"Aren't you glad, Nan? Aren't you terrible glad?"

"Why, of course I am, Flossie!"

"And aren't you glad, too, Bert?" Flossie Bobbsey, who had first asked this question of her sister, now paused in front of her older brother. She looked up at him smiling as he cut away with his knife at a soft piece of wood he was shaping into a boat for Freddie. "Aren't you terrible glad, Bert?"

"I sure am, Flossie!" Bert answered, with a laugh. "What makes you ask such funny questions?"

"Well, if you're glad why doesn't you wiggle like I do?" asked Flossie, without answering Bert. "I feel just like wigglin' and squigglin' inside and outside!" she added.

"Well, wiggle as much as you please, dear, but don't get your dress dirty, whatever you do," advised Nan, with the air of a little mother, for she felt that she must look after her smaller sister, since Mrs. Bobbsey was not there to do it.

"Oh, I won't get my dress dirty!" laughed Flossie. "'Cause if I do—"

"'Cause if you do you can't go to the picnic!" finished Freddie, who was so interested in watching brother Bert make the little wooden ship that he forgot all about talking.

"I'm just goin' to wiggle standin' up," Flossie said, and she did so, squirming about in delight at the fun which was soon to come.

"Don't forget your 'g' letters!" called Nan, shaking her finger at her sister. "You must say 'going' and 'standing' not 'goin',' my dear, or 'standin',' you know."

"Yes, I know. But when you feel like wigglin'—I mean wigglING," and Flossie said the last syllable very loudly, "why, then you don't think about 'g' letters; do you, Freddie?"

"I don't guess so," he answered, not taking his eyes off the knife that was flashing in Bert's hand, making the white slivers of wood scatter over the green grass.

"Oh, I just can hardly wait till the auto truck comes; can you, Nan?" asked Flossie, dancing over the lawn like a fairy in a play. "Oh, I'm so glad it doesn't rain!" and she looked anxiously up at the sky as if some cloud might float across the wonderful blue and spoil the day of pleasure.

"Yes, the weather is lovely," agreed Nan. "And if you don't think so much about it, Flossie, the truck will get here all the sooner."

"But I *like* to think about it!" cried Flossie. "It's the same as Christmas! The more you think about it the more fun it is! Oh, I'm going to look down the road and see if the truck is coming!"

Down toward the front gate she skipped, the big bow of ribbon on her hair flapping up and down like the wings of some great blue butterfly.

"Be careful about climbing on the gate!" warned Nan. "If you get rusty spots on your white dress they won't come out!"

"I'll be careful," Flossie promised, calling back over her shoulder, and, as she tripped along she sang: "We're going to a picnic! We're going to a picnic!"

"I think I'd better watch her so she won't soil her clothes," said Nan, getting up from a bench, where she had been sitting beside the boxes and baskets of lunch. "It would be too bad if she should get her dress dirty and couldn't go."

"I'm not going to get my clothes dirty, am I, Nan?" asked Freddie, as he looked at his white blouse.

"I hope not," Nan answered.

Suddenly there was an exclamation from Bert, as Nan started down the path toward Flossie.

"Ouch!" cried Bert.

"What's the matter?" Nan asked quickly.

"Cut myself!"

"Oh! Oh, dear!" screamed Freddie, who did not like the sight of the red blood which oozed from the end of his brother's finger.

"Oh, don't get any on my clean blouse, else I can't go to the picnic!"

Bert, who had popped the cut finger into his mouth as soon as he felt the hurt, now took it out to laugh.

"That's all you care about me, Freddie!" he joked. "I cut my finger, while making you a little boat, and all you care about is that I mustn't dirty your white blouse! I'll make you a lot more ships—I guess not!"

"Oh, but I am sorry for you!" Freddie declared. "Only I do so want to go to the picnic!"

"Yes, I know," Bert went on, seeing that Freddie was taking his talk too seriously. "I won't get any blood on you!"

"Is it much of a cut?" asked Nan "Do you want me to get the iodine?" Their Mother had taught the Bobbsey twins not to neglect hurts of this kind, and iodine, they knew, was good to "kill the germs," whatever that meant. Iodine smarted when put into a cut, but it was better to stand a little smart at first than a big pain afterward, so Daddy Bobbsey had said.

"Oh, it isn't much of a cut," Bert said. "I guess I don't need any iodine. You'd better go look after Flossie. The trucks may be along any time now, and we don't want to keep them waiting."

"All right. But you'd better not whittle any more on that boat or you may cut yourself so bad you can't go to the picnic."

"Let the boat go!" advised Freddie. "It's good enough, anyhow, and I want you to go to the picnic, Bert."

"All right. The little ship is almost finished, anyhow. I just have to make about three more cuts and then I'm done."

His finger had stopped bleeding—indeed the cut was a very small one—and Bert was soon putting the last touches to the tiny craft which Freddie wanted to sail in the little lake at the picnic grounds.

Just as Bert handed the homemade toy to his brother, and when Nan reached Flossie, in time to stop her from climbing on the gate, a noise of honking horns was heard down the street.

"Oh, here they come! Here come the trucks!" cried Flossie, dancing up and down.

"Get the lunch!" called Freddie, to make sure they would not go hungry on the picnic.

"I'll go in and tell mother we're going," called Nan to Bert, who shut up his knife, brushed the whittlings off his clothes, and began to gather up the boxes and baskets of lunch. "Watch Flossie!" Nan added, for there was no telling what the excitable little "fairy" might do at the last moment.

"All right," Bert answered. "Here, Freddie!" he called. "Don't run with that sharp-pointed boat in your hand. If you fall on it you'll get hurt."

"But I'm not going to fall!" said Freddie.

"You can't tell what you're going to do! Go easy!" Bert advised, and Freddie walked as slowly as he could to the gate where Flossie was eagerly gazing down the road.

The noise of the auto horns sounded more loudly, and soon two big trucks, filled with children and gay with flags, came into view. Boxes had been placed in the trucks for seats, and on these boxes, laughing, shouting, waving their hands and flags, were scores of happy, smiling boys and girls.

One of the trucks drew up at the gate of the house where lived the Bobbsey twins, the other auto keeping on, as it was well filled. But room had been saved in this one for Bert, Nan, Flossie and Freddie.

"Come on, Nan! Come on!" cried Flossie, still jumping up and down.

"Tell Nan to hurry!" added Freddie to his brother.

"She's coming," Bert said, as he walked down to the gate with the packages of lunch.

"Hello, Bert!" called Charlie Mason, from the truck. "Got enough to eat?"

"I guess so," Bert answered his chum, holding up the boxes and baskets. "Enough for two picnics I should say!"

"You can eat a lot when you're off in the woods," added Dannie Rugg. "It's like camping out."

"Here comes Nan!" exclaimed Grace Lavine, a particular chum of the older Bobbsey girl.

Nan, having hurried in to tell her mother the trucks had arrived, now hastened down the path, her hair flying in the wind.

"Have you everything? Take good care of Flossie and Freddie! Have a good time, and don't fall into the water!" Mrs. Bobbsey said, as she waved good-by to her twins while they clambered up into the truck.

"We will!" they answered.

"Good-by, Mother! Good-by!"

"Good-by, children!"

"Honk! Honk!" tooted the auto horn.

"All aboard!" called Nellie Parks. "All aboard!"

"I want to sit on the end!" declared Freddie, struggling to get in this position.

"You might fall out going up hill," said Bert. "I'll sit there, Freddie, and you can sit next me." The little fellow had to be content with this.

With children laughing, children singing, children shouting and children smiling, with flags flying and the horn tooting, the big auto started off, having taken aboard the Bobbsey twins; and soon the two trucks were out of sight around a turn in the road, bound for Pine Grove, on the outskirts of the town of Lakeport. It was the yearly picnic of one of the Lakeport Sunday schools.

"Isn't it a wonderful day?" asked Grace of Nan. The two friends and Nellie were sitting together.

"Yes, beautiful. We nearly always have a good day for the picnic."

"Did you bring any olives in your lunch. Nan?"

"Yes, and some dill pickles, too!"

"Oh, I just love dill pickles!" exclaimed Grace, "and we didn't have one in the house."

"I'll give you some of mine," offered Nan.

Flossie and Freddie were too excited, looking at sights along the road, to talk much, but they were as happy as if they had been chattering away like the others.

"Did your dog Snap bite your finger, Bert?" asked Dannie Rugg.

"No, my knife slipped when I was making Freddie a boat. Say, Freddie," he asked the little fellow, "did you lose your boat?"

"Nope, I have it here," and he held it up.

"Oh, all right."

On rumbled the trucks, raising clouds of dust. On each big auto were several grown folks, officers of the Sunday school, who were looking after the children. Some were fathers and mothers of the boys and girls.

Pine Grove was several miles outside the town of Lakeport, on the shores of a little lake. It was there the yearly picnics of the Sunday schools were always held, and the Bobbsey twins, as well as the other young people of the town, looked forward with pleasure to the outings.

"What you say we get up a ball game?" asked Dannie of Bert, when they were all settled in their places.

"Sure we will," Bert agreed. "Have we got enough fellows?"

"If you haven't, some of us girls will play," offered Nan.

"Pooh! Girls can't play ball!" sneered Charlie Mason.

"I can! I can bat a ball as far as you!" declared Nellie Parks.

"Maybe you can—if you can hit it!" admitted Charlie.

"I want to play ball!" chimed in Freddie. "I know how!"

"I guess if you sail your boat it will be all you want to do," said Bert, looking at his cut finger to see if it would hinder him from taking part in a game. He decided that it would not.

"We'll have lots of fun," said Dannie. "If we haven't enough for two nines we'll play a scrub game."

"Sure!" agreed Bert.

They were well out in the country now, and almost at the Grove. To reach it the trucks had to cross a bridge over a creek that flowed into Pine Lake, as the body of water was called.

The first truck passed over this bridge with a rumble like thunder. As it reached the other side Bert saw the driver of it lean from his seat, look back, and shout something to the driver of the truck on which the Bobbsey twins rode. What the man said Bert could not hear, and as he was wondering about it the second truck started over the bridge.

Suddenly there was a cracking of wood, a splintering, breaking sound, and the heavy truck, loaded with children, the Bobbsey twins among them, seemed to be sinking down.

"Oh, the bridge is breaking!" screamed Grace.

"We'll fall in the creek!" added Nellie.

There was a thundering sound as the auto driver turned on full power, and then, with another loud cracking noise, the truck came to a stop, and seemed to be sinking down through the breaking bridge!

"There's a Snake!"

With the first cries of alarm, Bert Bobbsey had jumped to his feet, one arm had gone out toward his sister Nan, and the other toward Flossie and Freddie. But no boy has arms long enough to reach for three relatives at once, especially when two of them, as Flossie and Freddie happened to be, were some distance away.

Bert did, however, manage to put one arm around Nan, and he pulled her toward him, though just why he hardly knew. As he did so there was a frightened movement on the part of all the other children aboard the truck, for they seemed to be sliding down toward the front of it.

"Oh, Bert! what has happened?" cried Nan. "Get hold of Flossie and Freddie, can't you?"

"I'm trying to," he answered.

"What's the matter?" Flossie called to Nan and Bert. "We're all slipping down!"

And this was just what was happening. The bridge over the stream seemed to have broken in the middle, just as the heavy truck got to that spot, and the auto's front wheels being lower than the rear ones, had slid the load of picnic merrymakers into a heap.

"Oh! Oh!" screamed Grace Lavine. "What is going to happen?"

"You'll be all right if you just keep quiet!" called the driver of the auto in a loud voice. "The bridge has only sagged a little! It isn't going to fall!"

This was good news provided it was true.

"All of you get off, and do it quietly," advised the driver. "You'll be all right."

"Are you sure?" asked Mrs. Simpson, one of the ladies in charge of the children.

"Oh, yes, ma'am. There's no danger," declared the man. He had jumped from his seat and was looking at the floor of the bridge under the front wheels of the truck.

"Keep quiet, every one!" ordered Mr. Blake, one of the gentlemen who had agreed to help the ladies look after the children. "Don't scream or cry, and move as quietly as you can. The easier you move the less danger there will be. The bridge hasn't quite broken in two yet."

But it was in grave danger of doing that, as Mr. Blake saw, and he was fearful that a bad accident would soon happen.

However, the thing to do now was to get all the children off the truck, over the bridge, and safe on solid ground. After that it might be possible to get the truck over and keep on to the picnic.

One by one the children, including the Bobbsey twins, started to get off the truck. They moved as carefully as they could, for they felt that they were like skaters on thin ice. The least quick movement might break something.

The truck that had gotten safely over the bridge had come to a stop, and children and grown folks were piling off it to see what they could do to save those in danger on the broken bridge.

And while the work of rescue is going on I will take a moment or two to tell my new readers something about the Bobbsey twins. Those of you who have read the other books in this series do not need to be introduced to Bert, Nan, Flossie and Freddie.

Those were the names of the four children. Bert and Nan were the older twins, and Flossie and Freddie the younger. You are first told about them in the book called "The Bobbsey Twins," and in that you learn that the Bobbsey family, consisting of Mr. and Mrs. Richard Bobbsey and their four children, lived in Lakeport, an eastern city on the shore of Lake Metoka, where Mr. Bobbsey had a lumber business.

In the family, though not exactly members of it, were Dinah, the jolly, fat, colored cook, and Sam Johnson, her husband. Then we must not forget Snap, the dog, and Snoop, the big cat.

Following the first book are a number of volumes telling of the adventures of the Bobbsey twins. They went to the country to visit Uncle Daniel, and at the seashore they had fun at the home of Uncle William. After that the Bobbseys enjoyed a trip in a houseboat, they journeyed to a great city, camped on Blueberry Island, saw the sights of Washington and even sailed to sea.

As if this was not enough Mr. and Mrs. Bobbsey took their children on a western trip among the cowboys, and just before the present story opens Bert and Nan, with Flossie and Freddie, had come back from Cedar Camp, where they had had some exciting adventures.

Now it was summer again, and one of the first delights of that season was the Sunday school picnic which had started off so well but which seemed likely now to end in an accident.

It was too bad that one truck should have gotten safely over the bridge, and that the other had to break through. The second truck was heavier than the first. The first may have cracked the bridge beams and the second one broken them.

"Careful now, children, careful!" warned Mr. Blake. "Don't jump down! Come to the end of the truck and I'll lift you down!"

"And as soon as you are down walk to the other side of the bridge; don't run—walk!" ordered the driver.

Bert remembered that it said this on the programs of the moving picture theaters, and he decided it was good advice.

One by one the children made their way up the sloping floor of the truck to the tailboard, and there Mr. Blake, Mrs. Simpson, and other men and women helped the little ones down.

"Oh, I feel like fainting!" sighed Grace.

"Don't be silly!" exclaimed Nan. "Nothing is going to happen!"

It was a good thing Nan felt this way, though, as a matter of fact, something dreadful might happen at any moment. If the cracked beams of the bridge should break all the way through, the auto would slide down into the water. And, though the creek was not very deep, still many would be hurt in the crash.

The Bobbsey twins, being nearest the rear of the auto, were among the first off. They did what the driver told them—walked quietly off the bridge.

At the farther end they joined the picnic party that had gotten off the first truck. And there, almost breathless, they watched the work of rescue going on.

One by one little boys and girls were lifted down off the truck, and then, when the last had reached safely the far shore, Mr. Blake, Mrs. Simpson, and the other men and women made their way carefully to land.

"Aren't you coming?" asked Mr. Blake of the truck driver, for the man was still close to his big car, looking at it and the sagging floor of the bridge.

"I want to see if I can get this truck off," he answered. "The machine isn't damaged any—it's only the bridge. I guess the load was too heavy for it."

"I heard it cracking as I went over," called the driver of the first truck. "I shouted a warning to you, but it was too late."

"Yes, it was too late to save the bridge, but maybe I can get my truck off," the other driver went on. "Anyhow, none of the children is hurt."

And this was so—something for which the Sunday school officers were very glad, indeed.

"If we had some pieces of wood to put under the bridge, to brace it up, maybe you could get the truck over," said the driver of the big auto that was safe on the far shore.

"Why don't you take fence rails?" asked Bert, who felt better, now that his sisters and brother were all right.

"Yes, we could do that," agreed the driver of the second auto. "Come on—give me a hand!" he called to his companion.

The two men worked away for a time, and braced up the bridge so that the auto could be driven carefully over it, though it was not easy to get it up the hill made when the bridge had sunk into the shape of the letter V.

But finally the empty second truck was safe on the other side of the stream, near the first one, and rails were put across the road to warn other vehicles not to try to cross the bridge. It was safe enough for a person to walk across, but it would not hold up an auto or a horse and wagon.

"We may as well go on to the picnic grounds," said Mr. Blake, when the smaller, frightened children had gotten over their crying.

"How we going to get home again if we can't cross the bridge?" asked Flossie, looking at the sagging structure.

"Oh, there's another bridge over the creek, about two miles down," the driver of the second truck said. "That will be all right."

Soon the children and grown folks were on the autos again, and moving toward the picnic grounds. This time there was not so much merry laughter and singing, for all felt that there had been a narrow escape from a terrible accident.

But gloom does not long remain with a party of jolly boys and girls, and by the time they alighted at Pine Grove each one was in high spirits again.

There were plenty of amusements at the picnic grounds. Little rustic pavilions here and there formed places where one could sit in the shade and eat lunch. There were swings for those who liked them, and boats for the older ones.

A green meadow, not far away, made a fine baseball field, and Bert, Charlie, and Dannie, with some of the older boys, at once made a rush for the field to start a baseball game.

"You take care of the lunch, Nan," Bert begged his older sister. "I'll come back when it's time to eat."

"Oh, I know that all right!" laughed Nan.

"Can't I play ball?" Freddie called, starting to follow Bert.

"You stay and sail your boat," Bert advised. "I made it for you to sail on the lake."

"That means I'll have to stay and watch him so he doesn't fall in," sighed Nan. "Well, you can't sail it all day, Freddie. I want to have some fun, too."

"You can sail it when I get tired," Freddie offered.

"I want to go in a big boat—a rowboat!" declared Flossie.

"I'll take you all for a row after the ball game," Bert promised, and Nan held this pleasure out to them to get them to do what she wanted.

The fun was now in full sway at the picnic grounds. Over in the meadow the boys were playing ball and shouting, and out on the little lake were many rowboats containing jolly parties. Some of the picnic folks had already started to eat their lunches.

"I'm hungry!" declared Freddie, seeing some children with sandwiches.

"So'm I!" added Flossie.

"Well, we can eat a little," decided Nan. She opened one of the smaller boxes, and took out a few sandwiches. "Let's go over under that tree and eat," she suggested, and soon they were sitting beneath a big pine tree, where the ground was covered with the smooth, brown needles.

Flossie had taken only a few bites of her sandwich when she suddenly jumped up and ran to Nan.

"Oh!" cried the little girl. "There's a snake! A snake!"

The Merry-go-round

Nan, though several years older than Flossie, was at first as much frightened by the cry of "a snake!" as was her little sister. Though Bert had often said only harmless snakes were in the woods around Lakeport, Nan could not help jumping up with a scream and pulling Flossie toward her.

"What's the matter?" asked Freddie, who had taken his sandwich a little distance away to eat.

"A snake! I saw a big snake!" cried Flossie again.

"Where is it?" asked Nan, for, as yet, she had caught no sight of any serpent.

"I—I almost sat on it," explained Flossie, clinging to Nan, and looking down over her shoulder.

Nan glanced toward where her sister had been sitting just before the alarm. She saw no wiggling snake crawling over the ground.

"Are you sure, Flossie?" Nan asked. "Are you sure you saw a snake?"

"Course I did. He almost put his head in my lap."

"Maybe he was hungry and wanted your sandwich," suggested Freddie. As he spoke he stepped forward to look at the place Flossie had pointed to as being the spot where she had seen the snake. And no sooner did Freddie take a step than Flossie cried:

"There it is again! Oh, the snake! The snake! Don't let him get me, Nan!"

Nan, too, saw something round and black moving near the place where Flossie had been sitting, and, fearing for the safety of her sister, the older Bobbsey girl lifted Flossie in her arms.

But no snake glided across the brown pine needles, and there was no hissing sound nor any forked tongue playing rapidly in and out, as Nan had once seen in a little snake Bert and Charlie Mason had caught.

"I don't believe there is a snake," Nan said, as Flossie slipped to the ground. "If there was one it has gone away."

"I'll hit him with a stone!" cried Freddie, turning to look for a rock. And as he moved Flossie cried again:

"There it is! I saw it move! That black thing!"

This time she pointed so carefully that Nan, letting her eye follow along Flossie's finger, saw what the little girl meant. And Nan laughed.

"Why, that isn't a snake!" she cried. "It's only a crooked, black tree branch! It does look a little like a snake, but it isn't really one, Flossie."

"But what made it move?" the little girl asked.

"I think it was Freddie, though he didn't do it on purpose," went on Nan. "Take another step, Freddie, as you did when you were looking for a stone."

Freddie moved a little and then they all saw what it was that had caused Flossie's fright. A long, dead branch of a tree lay on the ground. The larger end of it was close to where Flossie had been sitting with Nan, and this end did look somewhat like a snake, with a mouth and eyes. The middle of the stick was covered with pine needles, and the lower end stuck out beyond the needles and dried leaves close to where Freddie stood.

When the little boy took a step his foot touched the thin end of the branch, and made the thick end, near Flossie, move. Flossie took this for the swaying of a snake's head, and so she had screamed in fright.

"There's your snake—only a tree branch!" laughed Nan, as she lifted the dead limb and held it up.

"Ho! Ho!" laughed Freddie.

"Was that it—for sure?" asked Flossie.

"Of course!" answered Nan. "Come sit down and finish your sandwich. Then we'll play until it's time to eat our regular lunch."

"Well, I'm glad it wasn't a real snake," sighed Flossie, as she took her place with her sister beneath the tree.

"If it had been a real snake I'd 'a' pegged a rock at it!" boasted Freddie.

This was not the only fright at the picnic, for a little girl about Flossie's age cried when she saw a big frog in a pool, and a little boy ran screaming to his mother because a grasshopper perched on his shoulder.

But things like these always happen at picnics, and when the little frights were over even the children themselves laughed at their short-lived terror.

After the ball game Bert and Nan took the smaller Bobbsey twins for a row in a boat. Everything went well except that Freddie, in trying to sail his tiny ship over the side of the rowboat, nearly fell in himself. But Bert caught him just in time and pulled him back.

Then it was time for lunch, and what a good time all the children had, sitting at tables in the little rustic houses, or on the ground, eating from boxes and baskets. The Bobbsey twins, with a group of their friends, sat in a little pavilion by themselves.

Besides the lunch which each child or group of children brought, there was to be ice cream and cake, given by the Sunday school. The big freezers had been arranged in a sort of shed, and the cake and cream treat was to be given after the picnic lunches had been eaten. Just before the time for this part of the program, Mr. and Mrs. Bobbsey arrived at the grounds, driving over in the auto, as they had promised to do.

"Well, children, having fun?" asked the father of the Bobbsey twins.

"A dandy time!" exclaimed Bert. "My team won the ball game."

"And I 'most fell out of a boat!" boasted Freddie.

"Pooh! That's nothing! I 'most saw a snake!" exclaimed Flossie.

"A snake!" cried her mother.

"It wasn't real," Nan hastened to add, and Mrs. Bobbsey seemed to breathe easier.

"Well, you have had some excitement as well as fun," observed Mr. Bobbsey.

"Excitement!" cried Bert. "Say, Daddy, you ought to have been there when the truck almost smashed through the bridge!"

"Oh, did that happen?" exclaimed Mrs. Bobbsey.

"No, but almost," Bert went on.

"Well, it seems to me that everything 'almost' happened," said Mrs. Bobbsey. "Flossie *almost* saw a snake, Freddie *almost* fell overboard and the truck *almost* broke the bridge."

"Oh, the bridge really *is* broken," Nan said. And she told about that accident. Mr. and Mrs. Bobbsey had come to the picnic grounds by another road, and so had not seen the bridge that sagged in the middle.

"Well, all's well that ends well, so they say," remarked Mr. Bobbsey, "and we're glad you are having a good time. Yes, Mr. Blake, what is it?" he asked, for Mr. Blake, had come to where Mr. Bobbsey was talking to the children, and had called aloud.

"Do you want to help the ladies dish out the ice cream?" asked Mr. Blake.

"Surely!" answered the twins' father. "Wait until I take off my coat. Dishing out ice cream is rather messy work."

He removed his coat, hanging it on the limb of a tree near the shed where the ice cream freezers had been placed. Mrs. Bobbsey also offered to help, and when it became known that it was time for the ice cream and cake treat the picnic children began gathering at the rustic shed.

Before the dainties could be served, however, there came from down the road, in the opposite direction from the broken bridge, a low, rumbling sound.

"I hope it isn't going to rain," said Mrs. Morris, as she held a plate of ice cream in one hand.

"What makes you think it is?" Mrs. Bobbsey asked.

"Didn't you hear that thunder? I can't see the sky, on account of the trees, but I'm afraid it's clouding over."

"No, the sun is shining," said the twins' mother.

"But I'm sure that is thunder," went on Mrs. Morris.

There was a rumbling sound down the road, and there seemed to be some excitement there, for a number of children who had started toward the ice cream pavilion turned back.

"I wonder what it is," mused Mrs. Bobbsey. "I hope no 'almost' accidents are going to happen."

"I'll go see what it is," offered Bert.

He ran down the road, was gone a little while, and came back, his eyes shining with eagerness.

"Oh, it's a big merry-go-round!" he cried.

"A merry-go-round?" repeated his mother, busy at the ice cream.

"Yes, a man has a big merry-go-round in pieces on three or four big wagons," Bert reported. "Something's the matter with the engine—it runs by a steam engine, and something's the matter!"

"Bert, go call your father," said Mrs. Bobbsey, for her husband had gone to the far side of the grove to get another ice cream tub from the truck on which they were brought to the picnic. "We don't want any strange men setting up a merry-go-round here. Call your father!"

A Missing Coat

Mr. Bobbsey came hurrying over to the ice cream pavilion, with Bert almost running beside him to keep up with his father.

"What's all this, Mother?" asked Mr. Bobbsey, who, with his coat off and his sleeves rolled up, was working hard to help the ladies at the Sunday school picnic. "What's all this about a merry-go-round coming here?"

"I don't know that it is coming here," answered Mrs. Bobbsey, with a smile. "But some sort of affair is thundering along the road. You can see the crowd of children near it. A merry-go-round some one said. I thought perhaps some men owning one of those traveling affairs had heard about our picnic and had come here to set up a machine. We don't want anything like that."

"No," agreed Mr. Bobbsey with a smile. "We don't. I'll go see about it," and off he went, followed by Bert. Nan, with Flossie and Freddie, had already joined the group of children down near the road that extended along one edge of the picnic grove.

As Bert and his father neared the place, a loud, hissing sound was heard and a white cloud of steam shot into the air, while the little ones screamed and scattered.

"What's that?" cried Bert.

"I hope those youngsters don't go too near!" murmured Mr. Bobbsey. "The safety valve of his steam engine is blowing off. He's got too much pressure on. It may be dangerous," and Mr. Bobbsey broke into a run, which Bert imitated as well as he could with his shorter legs.

However, there was no great danger. As Mr. Bobbsey had said, the safety valve of a steam engine, on one of the trucks which carried the merry-go-round outfit, was blowing off, and a short, stout man, with a very red face, and a lanky boy, wearing ragged clothes, were working about the engine.

"Keep back, children! Keep back!" called Mr. Bobbsey, as he reached the road. "This merry-go-round isn't going to be set up here. Keep back out of danger!"

"That's what I wish they'd do, mister!" said the red-faced man in no very friendly voice. "They're under foot, and some of 'em may get stepped on. I've got trouble enough without a bunch of kids getting in the way."

He did not speak very nicely of children, Bert thought, and Nan was evidently of the same opinion from the way in which she looked at her brother. Flossie and Freddie thought nothing of this. They were too excited in looking at the merry-go-round outfit.

This fun-making machine was loaded on four large trucks, hauled by four sturdy horses each. On one truck was an engine, with a fire in it and smoke and steam coming from it. It was this that seemed to be causing the trouble which the red-faced man and the lanky boy were trying to make better.

Behind the engine truck, which was in the lead, were three other trucks, and the drivers of the horses kept to their seats, not offering to help the red-faced man.

The three trucks were piled high with the frame and roof of the merry-go-round. There were posts, boards, long iron rods, greasy cog wheels and all sorts of queer things. But what interested the children most were the wooden animals that made up the more showy part of the merry-go-round. There were horses, lions, tigers, camels, elephants, zebras, an ostrich and a cow.

"Oh, I want to ride on the cow!" cried Freddie.

"I'm going to get on the lion's back!" exclaimed Flossie.

"No, I want the lion, you can have the cow!" yelled Freddie. "I want the lion!"

"I had him first! I choosed him first an' he's mine! Daddy, can't I have the lion?" begged Flossie.

"Hush, children!" said Mr. Bobbsey, as Freddie opened his mouth to wail that he wanted the king of beasts. "The merry-go-round isn't going to be set up here. No one is going to get a ride."

"That's what, mister!" exclaimed the red-faced man. "I'm not going to stop here. I'm on my way to the Bolton County Fair with this merry-go-round outfit. I'm going to be there for a week or more. Just had a little trouble with this engine. I got steam up on it while on the road to see what the matter was."

"Is it fixed now?" asked Mr. Bobbsey.

"Yes, seems to be. Here, Bob," he called to the lanky boy, "haul the fire now, and we'll let her cool down. I guess she'll work now. Got up a good steam pressure, anyhow."

The ragged boy did something to the engine, when suddenly a burst of melody struck on the ears of all, and from an organ there was ground out a gay dancing tune.

"Oh, music!" cried Flossie.

"Where's the hand organ monkey?" Freddie wanted to know.

"I'm going to get Grace and we can dance!" exclaimed Nan, for she and her chums did simple little dances at school.

"I want to see the monkey!" wailed Freddie again.

"There isn't any monkey," Bert said. "It isn't exactly a hand organ. It's one that works by steam, I imagine," he said. "It's part of the merry-go-round."

"That's right. It's a good organ, too," said the ragged, lanky boy, who was working away at the engine, while the red-faced man had started for the front of the truck. Hearing the melody the red-faced man turned to the boy and angrily cried:

"Here! I didn't tell you to turn that music on! Shut it off, do you hear!"

"My, what a cross man!" said Flossie, in what she meant to be a whisper.

"Hush!" her father said.

"Shut that organ off! What'd you turn it on for, Bob?" grumbled the man.

"I didn't turn it on, Mr. Blipper. It turned itself on—too much steam, I guess."

"Well, shut it off, do you hear! I don't want to play music when I don't get any money for it. Shut it off!"

The boy did something to the engine and the organ music died away in a sad wail.

"Oh, dear!" sighed Flossie.

"Now we can't have any dance," lamented Nan.

"How long are you going to stop here, Mr.—er—did I understand your name was Blipper?" asked Mr. Bobbsey, thinking he might arrange to have the organ played a little while for the children.

"Blipper is my name—Aaron Blipper," answered the man. "Sole owner and proprietor of Blipper's Merry-Go-Round which will exhibit for a week, and maybe more, at the Bolton County Fair."

"My name is Bobbsey," went on the father of the twins. "Your name and mine have the same first letter, anyhow. I was going to say that if you were going to remain here a while I'd give you a dollar to let the organ play for the children. This is a Sunday school picnic."

"I guessed it was," said Mr. Blipper. "Well, if you was to give me a dollar I'd have Bob turn the music on again. I think a dollar will pay for what coal I burn in the engine. The organ is worked by the engine. I can't turn it by hand, or I'd let Bob do that. But I'll play for a dollar."

"Here you are then," said Mr. Bobbsey, and he passed over a bill.

"Turn the organ on, Bob!" ordered Mr. Blipper. "And while we're waiting here get a pail and water the horses. Might as well make yourself useful as well as ornamental."

To the Bobbsey twins it seemed that Bob had been making himself busy, if not useful, ever since the merry-go-round had halted near the picnic grounds.

The boy turned a handle and once more the organ began grinding out music of one kind or another. It was not very good, of course, but it pleased the children. Soon Flossie and Freddie were dancing on the green grass beside the road, and Nan and many of the other children were also enjoying themselves in this way. Though it was a Sunday school picnic, such simple dances as the children did could not be found fault with by any one.

Bert and his especial chums did not dance. They walked about the trucks of the merry-go-round, looking at the wooden animals. Mainly, however, they were interested in the steam engine which not only turned the machine around, once it was set up, but also played the organ.

"I'd like to see this thing going," said Charlie Mason.

"So would I," agreed Dannie Rugg.

"Maybe my father will take me to the Bolton County Fair," remarked Bert. "If he does I'll have a ride."

Then the ragged boy, who had been watering the horses, while the drivers dozed on their high seats, came up with an empty pail. He looked at the engine, changed the organ so that it played a different tune and let some hot water run out of a little faucet.

"Do you know how to run the engine?" asked Bert.

"Sure I do!"

"What's your name?" asked Charlie.

"Bob."

"Bob what?" Dannie wanted to know.

"Bob Guess."

"Bob Guess! That's a queer name," remarked Bert.

"Well, it isn't exactly my real name," the ragged lad went on. "I'm an orphan. I haven't had any real folks in a long time. I was taken out of the asylum by this man, so he says. He adopted me, I reckon, and he said he gave me that name 'cause he had to *guess* what my real name was. So I'm called Bob Guess."

"A queer name," murmured Bert. "But I'd like to know how to work a steam engine."

"So'd I!" agreed the other boys.

"Pooh! It's easy," said Bob Guess, who seemed to like to show off. For he turned another little faucet, thereby sending out a cloud of steam, and causing Charlie Mason to jump back.

"Don't be skeered! It won't hurt you!" laughed Bob.

"Isn't it hot?"

"Not after it comes from the boiler. Look, I can hold my hand right in it," which Bob Guess did, letting a cloud of steam envelop both his rather dirty hands.

"Whew!" whistled Dannie, in amazement.

"I'm going to try it!" said Bert, rightly guessing that at a short distance from the faucet the steam cooled off; which was true, as you know if you have ever "felt" of the steam coming from a house radiator on a cold day.

But as Bert stretched out his hand to test the steam as Bob had done, Mr. Blipper called from where he stood talking to the driver of the last truck.

"Stop monkeying with that engine, Bob!" yelled the red-faced man. "You want to get it all out of kilter again!"

"I was only testin' the steam gauge," the boy answered.

"Well, you let it alone, do you hear, and water the horses."

"I have watered 'em!"

"Well, water 'em some more! I'm not going to stop again till I get to the Bolton County Fair if I can help it."

"He's sort of cross, isn't he?" asked Charlie, as Bob moved off.

"More than that—he's mean!" declared the ragged lad.

Bert and his chums stood looking at the steam engine and listening to the organ, while Nan and the smaller children danced. Then up came Mr. Blipper.

"I guess this is a dollar's worth of music," he announced.

"I believe so," agreed Mr. Bobbsey, with a smile. "The children have enjoyed it. Thank you!"

"Um!" grunted Mr. Blipper. "Here you, Bob!" he roared. "Come and shut off this steam. We're going to travel!"

He climbed up on the seat, and Bob, after hanging the water pail on a hook beneath the truck, shut off the engine. The organ ceased playing, and the trucks containing the merry-go-round lumbered off.

"Good-by!" called the Bobbsey twins.

"Good-by!" echoed Bob Guess.

"I wonder if we'll ever see him again," murmured Bert.

And he was to see the strange lad again, under queer circumstances.

"Come, children, your ice cream will get cold!" called Mrs. Bobbsey, who had come from the pavilion to summon the little guests.

"Ice cream get cold! Ha! Ha!" laughed Grace Lavine.

"I like mine cold," chuckled Dannie Rugg.

Back across the fields ran the merry, laughing children. The Sunday school picnic, in spite of the danger at the bridge, had turned out most wonderfully.

Soon the caravan of the merry-go-round was but a series of faint specks down the dusty road. It was taking a route that would not take it across the broken bridge.

The Bobbsey twins and their friends sat about eating ice cream and cake, and some of them talked about the strange boy and the organ that was played by steam.

"I'm going to have an organ like that when I grow up," said Freddie.

"An' I'm goin' to help you play it, an' ride on a lion," added Flossie, and the others laughed.

Picnics, however delightful, cannot go on forever, and this one came to an end as the afternoon shadows were falling. Mr. Bobbsey had been very busy helping his wife and the other ladies, and now, as the time came for him to go home in the small auto in which he and his wife had ridden to the grove, he rolled down his sleeves, and looked about him.

"What are you after?" his wife asked.

"My coat. I hung it on a tree limb right here, I thought."

"Yes, I saw you," said Nan.

"But it isn't here now!" her father went on.

"Here's some sort of coat," announced Bert, picking up one from the ground under a tree near the ice cream pavilion.

"That's where I hung my coat," said Mr. Bobbsey. "And this coat isn't mine. Mine was a good, new one. This is an old, ragged one. Dear me! I hope my coat hasn't been stolen! It had some money in one pocket, and also some papers I need at the lumber office! Where is my coat?"

Sam Is Worried

While fathers, mothers, and other relatives were gathering up their own children, or children of whom they had charge, to see that they were safely loaded into the two big trucks to go home from the picnic, the Bobbsey twins—at least Bert and Nan—were searching for their father's coat. Flossie and Freddie were too small to pay much attention to anything of this sort. The smaller twins were talking about the merry-go-round and starting over again the dispute as to who should ride on the wooden lion.

"Are you sure you left your coat hanging on the tree limb?" asked Mrs. Bobbsey.

"I'm certain of it," her husband answered. "And this old coat never was mine—I wouldn't own it!"

He dropped to the ground the ragged garment that had been found lying beneath the tree.

"I thought maybe you had hung your coat over by the ice cream shed," went on Mrs. Bobbsey. "You may have done that and have forgotten about it."

"No, I didn't do that," said the father of the Bobbsey twins. "I remember hanging my coat on the tree, for I recall noticing what a regular hook, like one on our rack at home, a broken piece of the branch made. My coat was here. But it's gone now, and this old one is left in place of it."

There was no question about that. Search as Mr. and Mrs. Bobbsey and the children did, over the picnic grounds, the lumberman's coat, with money in one pocket and papers in another, was gone.

"Who do you s'pose could have taken it?" asked Nan, as her father looked about him with a puzzled air.

"I don't know," he answered, "unless—"

"Maybe it was tramps!" interrupted Bert.

"There weren't any tramps here on our picnic grounds," said Mrs. Bobbsey. "Some of the drivers of the merry-go-round trucks looked like tramps, but they didn't get off their seats, did they?"

"Not that I noticed," her husband answered. "Well, there's no use looking farther. My coat is gone—stolen I'm afraid. This old one is left in its place. I haven't any use for this," and he kicked it to one side. "Never mind. It isn't cold. I can ride home without a coat."

"There's a lap robe in the auto," Mrs. Bobbsey said. "You can wrap that about you if you get chilly on the way home."

"Yes," agreed Mr. Bobbsey, "I can do that. Trot along, Bobbsey twins. Get into your picnic truck, and we'll see who gets home first."

"Like Little Red Riding Hood and the Wolf," laughed Flossie.

While Mr. and Mrs. Bobbsey walked over to where Mr. Bobbsey had left the runabout auto in which he and his wife had come to the picnic grounds, Bert, Nan, and the other children took their places in the big truck.

"Merrily we roll along—roll along—roll along!"

Some one started that song as the trucks rumbled out of the picnic grove. On account of the broken bridge a different road home had to be taken; a longer one. Having a lighter car than the trucks, Mr. Bobbsey and his wife could go faster than the loads of merry-makers, and the twins waved good-by to their parents, who were soon lost to sight.

"I guess they'll get home first," said Nan to Bert.

"I guess so—I Bob Guess so!" he added, making a joke on the name of the strange lad who had worked the steam organ of the merry-go-round.

"I feel sorry for that boy," said Nan. "Mr. Blipper was so cross and mean to him."

"Yes, he was cross," agreed Bert. "I hope daddy finds his coat," he added. "It's funny to have a coat stolen at a Sunday school picnic."

"Maybe somebody took it by mistake," suggested his sister.

"I don't believe they would, and leave an old ragged coat in place of a good one," Bert remarked.

"Maybe not," said Nan.

The picnic party was rather more quiet on the journey home than it had been on the way to Pine Grove. The reason was that the children were tired, and some of them sleepy. They sang for a while after leaving the grove, Bert and Nan starting many melodies in which the others joined.

But finally the songs died away, and about the only noise that was heard was the rumble of the big trucks.

"Do we have to cross any bridges?" asked Mrs. Morris, of the driver of the auto in which she rode with the Bobbsey twins.

"One bridge—yes, lady," was the answer.

"Dear me! I hope it doesn't break down as the white one did to-day," exclaimed the nervous little lady.

"No danger. It's a big iron one," said the driver.

"I'm glad of that," went on Mrs. Morris. "I'm always worried when I cross a bridge."

But there were no more accidents. The trucks took a little longer returning to Lakeport than they had making the trip earlier in the day, for they had to go a roundabout way. But finally the outskirts of the town were reached, and the children began getting off as they neared their homes.

"Good-by! Good-by!" they called one to another.

Finally the home of the Bobbsey twins came in sight in the early summer evening.

"Good-by, Bert and Nan!" called their chums.

"Good-by, Flossie and Freddie!"

"Good-by! Good-by!" echoed the Bobbsey twins.

"Dad is home ahead of us," remarked Bert to Nan, as they went up the steps.

"How do you know?" asked Nan.

"Because I see the runabout there," and Bert pointed toward the garage. "Seems to be something wrong," Bert went on. "Mother is there and so is Sam."

"Let's go see what it is," suggested Nan, as Dinah came to the door, calling: "Am mah honey lambs safe an' sound?"

"Yes, Dinah!" said Freddie. "And I'm hungry, too!"

"Ah spects yo' is, honey! Ah spects yo' is!" laughed the jolly, fat cook. "Come right in yeah an' hab some cake!"

"I'm going to ride on a lion, I am!" stated Flossie.

"Good lan', chile! A lion!" exclaimed Dinah, raising her hands in surprise. "Yep! A lion!"

"Oh, mah honey lamb! Don't yo' do no sich a thing!" cried Dinah. "A lion done eat yo' laigs off!"

"'Tisn't a real lion. I mean a wooden lion on a merry-go-round like we saw to-day," Flossie explained.

"Oh, a wooden lion!" and Dinah laughed. "Well, come in yeah, honey lambs, an' I'll feed yo'. Ah'll make beliebe yo' all is hungry lions, an' Ah'll feed yo'!"

And while Flossie and Freddie went into the house with Dinah, Bert and Nan hurried toward the garage, where they saw their father and mother talking with Sam Johnson.

"I's done suah I put dat lap robe in de auto," said Dinah's husband.

"I thought you did, Sam," said Mrs. Bobbsey. "Yet when Mr. Bobbsey looked for it, to put around him, as he had no coat, the robe was gone."

"Are you sure it isn't in the garage, Sam?" asked Mr. Bobbsey.

"Sartin suah, sah! I done put it in de little auto when yo' all started off, 'case I reckoned it'd be dusty."

"Well, the lap robe is gone like my coat," said Mr. Bobbsey. "Too bad, for it was a new one."

"It suah am too bad!" declared Sam. "Yo' all has me worried!"

"Well, you don't need to worry, Sam," said Mrs. Bobbsey kindly. "It isn't your fault. I know you put the robe in the auto, for I saw it when we started. But when I wanted it to wrap around Mr. Bobbsey, after his coat was taken, and it was cool riding home, the robe was gone."

"Stolen, Mother, do you think?" asked Nan.

"I wouldn't say that. It may have fallen out on the way."

"Well, that's two things gone the same day," said Mr. Bobbsey, who was still in his shirt sleeves, as he had come from the picnic. "My coat and the lap robe. I guess that Blipper's merry-go-round, which is to show at the Bolton County Fair, didn't bring me any good luck."

Bert and Nan were wondering if Bob Guess or the red-faced man knew anything of their father's coat and the missing lap robe when from the kitchen Dinah's voice excitedly called:

"Come heah! Come heah if yo' please, Mr. Bobbsey! Suffin's done gone an' happened!"

"Oh, dear!" cried Mrs. Bobbsey. "What's the matter now?"

Happy Days Coming

When Dinah called in this fashion, with worry making itself heard in her voice, Mrs. Bobbsey always hurried to see what the matter was. Generally it was something the smaller Bobbsey twins had done. And as she knew Flossie and Freddie were now in the kitchen, Mother Bobbsey feared one of the smaller children had been hurt.

"What is it, Dinah?" asked the mother, as she hurried back toward the house. Bert and Nan, with their father, waiting only a moment, followed Mrs. Bobbsey.

"I should think Freddie and Flossie would have had enough fun at the picnic not to want to do any more cutting up," remarked Nan.

"You never can tell what those tykes will do," observed Bert. "I don't hear either of 'em yelling, and that's a good sign."

But just as he spoke there came a wail from the kitchen, which, by this time, Mrs. Bobbsey had reached, disappearing within.

"That's Flossie," said Nan.

Again came the voice of a little child, crying either in fear or in delight at some funny happening, it could not be told which.

"There goes Freddie, letting off steam," said Bert. "I guess it isn't anything very much. Freddie always laughs in that squealing way when something tickles him."

Mr. Bobbsey, with the two older twins, entered the kitchen soon after Mrs. Bobbsey. There stood Flossie and Freddie before a low kitchen table, one leaf of which was down, so that whatever was under could not be seen very well, on account of the shadow cast by the electric light. And beside Flossie and Freddie stood Dinah.

"What's the matter?" asked Mr. Bobbsey.

"Dinah says Snoop, our cat, has caught some sort of animal and has it under the table," said Mrs. Bobbsey.

"It's a big animal and it's got fur on," declared Flossie, greatly excited.

"An' it's got yellow eyes and four legs an' it's long—it's as long as my arm!" added Freddie, his eyes big with wonder. "Oh, it was awful funny!" he went on, squealing with delight. "I saw Snoop drag it under the table and I called Dinah. Didn't I, Dinah?"

"Dat's whut yo' done, honey lamb! Ah don't know whut it is Snoop has, Mis' Bobbsey," went on the colored cook, "but it's some sort o' animile!"

"And Snoop growled, he did, when he dragged it under the table!" exclaimed Flossie. "I heard Snoop growl, I did! Listen!"

Surely enough the cat growled again, just as a lion or a tiger in the jungle would growl after catching its dinner—only not so loud, of course.

"Oh!" murmured Flossie, making a dive for her mother's skirts.

"There! Look! I saw its tail!" cried Freddie.

As he spoke just a flash of some furry animal was seen under the table where Snoop had gone to hide.

"I hope it isn't a little skunk!" exclaimed Mrs. Bobbsey.

"Don't worry!" advised her husband. "If it was a young skunk that Snoop had, you'd have known it long before this. And Snoop never would try to catch a skunk—Snoop would know better."

"But what is it? He has something!" insisted Mrs. Bobbsey.

"Maybe I can coax Snoop out," put in Nan. "He minds me better than he does any one else. Here, Snoop! Come on out, nice Snoop!" she called in a gentle voice.

But Snoop only growled in answer, and seemed to be shaking, beneath the table, the unknown animal he had caught and dragged there.

"Shall I get the rake and pull him out?" asked Bert.

"No, you might hurt him," replied Mr. Bobbsey. "Go out to the garage and get the big flash lamp from Sam. I can shine that under the table and we can see what it is before we do anything. Evidently Snoop isn't going to come out until he gets ready. And it may be he has a large rat or—"

Dinah gave a scream.

"Oh—a rat!" she cried.

"Maybe it's only a little mouse—I like a funny little mouse," said Flossie.

"Well, I don't," said Dinah. "They eats mah food."

"Maybe it's only a little mole from the garden," went on Mr. Bobbsey.

"It's bigger'n a ground mole!" declared Freddie. "I saw it, an' it's long and brown and has legs an' brown eyes that shine."

"Well, whatever it is it can't be very dangerous," said Mr. Bobbsey. "If it was, Snoop never would have dared to get it. But I don't want to reach under there in the dark and perhaps get bitten and scratched by Snoop, or whatever he has. We'll wait for the flash light."

Bert now came running in with this, Sam following when he heard that the cat had something strange under the table in the kitchen.

"Dey suah am lots ob t'ings happenin' dis day," observed Sam.

Mr. Bobbsey flashed the light under the table. The four twins had stooped down to get a better view, and Freddie cried:

"I see its eyes shining!"

"I can see its tail! Oh, no, that's Snoop's tail!" added Flossie.

"Snoop, what have you there? Stop growling and give it to me!" demanded Mr. Bobbsey, thrusting his hand under the table.

"Be careful," advised his wife. "It may bite."

Mr. Bobbsey laughed and thrust his hand farther under the table. There was a little scuffle as Snoop tried to hold fast to what he had. He clung so hard to it with teeth and claws that he was dragged over the smooth linoleum on the floor.

"Here's your wild beast!" cried Mr. Bobbsey, as he arose, and held something covered with brown fur dangling from one hand.

"What is it?" asked Mrs. Bobbsey. "That's not a rat."

"No, it's your fur neck piece," her husband said, with a laugh.

"Oh, I wore it to the picnic, for I thought it would be cool coming home," said Mrs. Bobbsey, as she took the piece of fur. "And I laid it on the hall table. I forgot about Snoop. He must have seen it, thought it was a strange animal, and carried it away with him. Oh, Snoop!" and she shook her finger at the cat which, now that it had nothing to play with, came out from beneath the table.

"It does look like an animal," said Nan.

And indeed the fur piece did. For it was fashioned with an imitation of an animal's head, with yellow glass eyes. The fur piece was quite long and four little legs were fastened to it. So that it is no wonder a cat, or even a boy or a girl, at first look, would take it for something real.

"Well, Snoop had a good time with it, while it lasted," said Mr. Bobbsey, with a laugh.

"And my fur wouldn't have lasted much longer with him, if he'd started to claw and bite it," remarked Mrs. Bobbsey. "I'm glad you called me in, Dinah."

"Yessum, Ah thought maybe yo'd better see what the cat had, 'cause Ah couldn't make out what 'twas," the cook answered.

"Well, now that the excitement is over, we'd better have supper," said Mr. Bobbsey. "Or did you youngsters have enough at the picnic to last until morning?"

"We want to eat now!" decided Bert. "That wasn't so much we had at the picnic."

"I guess you were extra hungry, from being out of doors all day," his mother said. "Well, supper will soon be ready."

As they ate they talked over the fun they had had at Pine Grove, and Flossie remarked:

"I'm going to ride on a wooden lion, I am—on the merry-go-round. I'm going to ride on the lion."

"So'm I," declared Freddie. "There are two lions, an' I'm going to ride on one an' Flossie on the other one."

"Where's your merry-go-round?" asked Nan.

"At the fair—the Bolton County Fair," said Freddie. "I heard that funny red-faced man say so."

"But the Bolton Fair is a long way off," went on Nan.

"Daddy will take us; won't you?" asked Flossie. "Can't we go to the fair and ride on the merry-go-round?" she teased.

"Well, I don't know," answered Mr. Bobbsey slowly. "I suppose it would be a good thing to visit a big county fair, and this is one of the largest."

"But we'd have to go and stay for some time," said Mrs. Bobbsey. "Bolton is a long way off. We couldn't go and come the same day."

"One ought to spend more than a day at a big fair if he wants to see everything," went on Mr. Bobbsey. "I never could stay as long as I wanted to when I was a boy. Now, I was thinking perhaps we could all go to Meadow Brook Farm for a little visit. From Meadow Brook it isn't far to the Bolton County Fair."

"Oh, let's go!" cried Bert and Nan.

"What about school?" asked their mother.

"School doesn't open until later this fall than usual," explained Mr. Bobbsey. "They are repairing the school house and the work will not be finished in time for the regular fall opening. I know, for the school board buys lumber of me.

"So, as long as the children don't have to be back until the middle of October, we could all go to Meadow Brook, and from there visit the fair. Would you like that?" he asked his wife.

"I think it would be lovely!"

"So do I!" echoed the Bobbsey twins.

"Well, then, we'll think about it," promised their father. "You will have some happy days to think about until it is time to go. And now I think it is time for my little Fairy and my brave Fireman to go to bed." Daddy Bobbsey sometimes called the small twins by these pet names. "Come on! Up to bed!" he called. "We'll talk more about the Bolton County Fair another day!"

As he was carrying the smaller children up to bed, a style of travel the little twins loved, there came a ring at the front door bell. Dinah, who answered, came back to say:

"Dere's a p'liceman outside whut wants to see yo', Mr. Bobbsey."

"A policeman?"

"Yas, sah!"

"A policeman for me?"

"Yas, sah!"

"Dear me!" Mr. Bobbsey murmured. "What can be the matter now!"

"Oh, Daddy!" squealed Flossie, at once filled with excitement.

"What do you suppose—" began Bert, and then stopped in the midst of his speech.

"Maybe he has found your lost coat," suggested Nan, as her father put Flossie and Freddie down in an easy chair.

The Crying Boy

There had been so much excitement over the strange "animal" which Snoop had under the table that, for a time, the Bobbsey twins had forgotten about their father's coat having been taken at the picnic. Nor had they remembered about the missing lap robe. But now, as Nan said this, every one—except perhaps the smaller twins—thought about the things that were gone.

"Oh, that's so!" exclaimed Bert, following what his sister said. "Maybe the policeman has come to bring back your lost coat, Daddy!"

"I hope he has," said Mr. Bobbsey. "Not only do I not want to lose the coat, for a suit of clothes isn't of much use without a coat, but I don't like to lose the money and papers."

"No, sah, Mr. Bobbsey, de p'liceman didn't hab no coat," said Dinah.

"He didn't?" remarked Mr. Bobbsey.

"No, sah. He didn't."

"Well then, I can't imagine what he wants," went on the father of the Bobbsey twins. "Ask him to come in, Dinah."

In came the policeman. He was one the children knew, from having often seen him pass the house.

"Good evening, Mr. Bobbsey," said the officer, the light flashing on his brass buttons. "I came up to see about a lap robe stolen from your auto."

"Did you find it?" asked Mrs. Bobbsey. "I'm so glad! And did you find Mr. Bobbsey's coat, also?"

"Why, no, Mrs. Bobbsey, I didn't," answered Policeman Murphy. "I didn't know about any lost coat. I was just sent up from the police station to inquire about the robbery of a lap robe. Somebody telephoned down that a policeman was wanted because a lap robe had been stolen. That's why I came up—because of the telephone message."

"Telephone!" exclaimed Mr. Bobbsey. "I didn't telephone for you, Mr. Murphy."

"Neither did I," said Mrs. Bobbsey. "Perhaps it was one of the children," and she looked at Bert and Nan.

The older Bobbsey twins shook their heads. Flossie and Freddie, though they knew how to telephone, would hardly have thought of calling up the police. But they were asked about it.

"Nope, we didn't do it," Flossie said. "Though we likes p'licemans; don't we, Freddie?"

"Yeppie," he answered sleepily. "When I grows up I'm goin' be a p'licemans or a firesmans—I forget which."

"He's sleepy," laughed the officer. "But what about this, Mr. Bobbsey? Some one must have telephoned."

"Yes, of course. I wonder if it could have been Mr. Blipper or that lad who called himself Bob Guess?"

"Who are they?" the officer asked.

"Mr. Blipper is a man who owns a merry-go-round he takes to fairs and circuses. He passed the picnic grounds where we were to-day. He's on his way to the Bolton County Fair. He had with him a boy named Bob Guess—called that because the lad is an orphan and they had to 'guess' at his name. Soon after this Blipper and his outfit left, I missed my coat, and, coming home, we found the lap robe gone. I was going to ride after him, but we had a little excitement here, and I haven't had a chance. Then you came along and—"

The sound of steps was heard on the side porch, and in came Sam, quite excited.

"'Scuse me!" he murmured, as he entered. "Oh, de p'liceman done come!" he exclaimed. "He's heah! I'm glad!"

"Did you expect him?" asked Mr. Bobbsey.

"Yes, sah, Mr. Bobbsey, I did! When de lap robe was gone I t'ought maybe you t'ink I might 'a' been careless like, an' let some chicken t'ieves in. So I telephoned fo' a p'liceman to come an' see if he could cotch de burglar!"

"Oh, Sam, you didn't need to do that!" exclaimed Mrs. Bobbsey. "We know it wasn't your fault that the lap robe was taken, any more than it was that Mr. Bobbsey's coat was stolen."

"Of course not!" echoed her husband.

"Well, I t'ought better we have a p'liceman," murmured Sam.

"I don't know what there is for him to do," said Mr. Bobbsey. "As nearly as I can figure it out, my coat was stolen at the picnic grounds and the lap robe was taken about the same time."

"It was," agreed Mrs. Bobbsey. "And I think that Blipper—or perhaps Bob Guess—had something to do with both thefts."

"It might be," replied the officer. "Those traveling show people aren't very careful, sometimes. I'll report back to the chief and see what he says. If we get sight of this merry-go-round crowd, Mr. Bobbsey, we'll stop them and ask them about your coat and the robe."

"Thank you, I wish you would. But I don't imagine you'll see them. They are on their way to Bolton, and we shall be there ourselves next week, so we can make some inquiries."

Officer Murphy left, finding there was nothing he could do. Flossie and Freddie were carried up to bed, and Nan danced about the room, singing:

"We're going to the fair! We're going to the fair! We're going to the Bolton County Fair!"

And Bert echoed:

"Maybe we'll find daddy's coat when we get there!"

Then, tired but happy over their fun at the picnic and too sleepy to worry much over the lost articles, the Bobbsey twins at last went to bed.

As their parents had said, school would not open as early that fall as in other years, because some rebuilding work was being done in a few of the rooms. So there was time to go to Meadow Brook, and from there to visit Bolton, a few miles away, where the big fair was being held.

"Do you really think we can go, Mother?" asked Nan, the next day.

"I don't see why not. Your father seems to have made up his mind to it."

"Well, I hope he doesn't change it, as he does sometimes," said Bert, with a laugh. "They're going to have airships and a balloon at the fair, Charlie Mason says, and maybe I can go up in the balloon. Wouldn't that be great, Nan?"

"I'm not going up in any balloon!"

"I am!" decided Bert, as if that was all there was to it.

"An' I'm going to ride on a lion!" cried Flossie.

"So'm I!" chimed in her brother Freddie.

Uncle Daniel Bobbsey and his wife Sarah, with their son Harry, lived at Meadow Brook Farm. The Bobbsey twins had been there more than once, as those who have read the other books of this series will remember. And now it was proposed to go there again.

"But we'll be at the fair more than we will be at Meadow Brook, sha'n't we?" asked Nan of her father.

"Well, sort of betwixt and between," he answered, with a laugh.

Uncle Daniel having been written to, said he would be delighted to have his brother and his brother's family come out for the remainder of the summer and early fall. And in about a week all preparations were made.

The trip was to be made in the Bobbsey's big auto, and would take about a day. By starting early in the morning Meadow Brook Farm could be reached by night. From there it was only a short distance to Bolton where, each year, a big fair was held.

"And if I see that Bob Guess I'll make him tell where daddy's coat is!" declared Bert.

"And the lap robe, too!" added Nan.

It was a fine, sunny day when the start was made. Into the auto piled the Bobbsey twins, with boxes and baskets of lunch.

"It's like another picnic!" laughed Nan, as she saw Bert piling away the good things to eat.

"Hab a good time, honey lambs!" called fat Dinah, as she and her husband stood on the steps, waving good-by.

"Take good care of Snoop and Snap!" begged Nan.

"We will!" promised Sam.

Snap, the dog, wanted to come along, but as he could not very well be looked after on this trip he had to be left behind, much to his sorrow. He howled dismally as the auto went down the road.

Not very much happened on the way to Meadow Brook. Once a tire was punctured and Mr. Bobbsey had to stop to put on a spare one. But this happened near a garage, so he had a man from there do the work, while he and his wife, with the twins, went into a little grove of trees and ate lunch.

"Be careful of your coat!" warned Mrs. Bobbsey, as her husband took it off and hung it on a tree while he built a fire to heat the water for tea.

"Oh, no one is going to steal this one!" he said. "Anyhow, it's an old one. But there's no one here to take it. No Mr. Blipper or Bob Guess around now."

"Well, don't forget, and go off, leaving it hang on the tree," warned his wife.

"I won't," said Mr. Bobbsey.

A fire was made, and as Mrs. Bobbsey was sitting with her back against a stump, comfortably sipping her tea, she heard the sound of crying. As Bert and Nan, with Flossie and Freddie, were gathering flowers not far away, Mrs. Bobbsey could see that it was none of her twins who was sobbing.

But the crying kept up, and she looked around to see whence it came. Mr. Bobbsey was busy packing up the lunch things, for there was enough food left to serve a little tea around five o'clock, since Meadow Brook Farm would not be reached before seven o'clock that evening, on account of the delay over the tire.

"Who is that crying, Dick?" asked Mrs. Bobbsey.

"Crying? Why, I don't hear—yes, I do, too!" her husband added, as the sound of sobs came to his ears. He looked to make sure his own children were all right and then glanced about.

As he did so there came from a little clump of trees, not far from the grove where the Bobbseys had eaten lunch, a ragged boy, who seemed in pain or distress, for he was crying very hard.

"Oh, the poor lad!" said Mrs. Bobbsey in a kind voice. "Go see what the matter is, Dick! He is in trouble of some sort! I wonder who he is?"

"Yes, without doubt, the lad's in trouble. We'll see what we can do," answered the father of the twins.

The crying boy walked slowly toward the Bobbsey family, and now the twins, hearing his sobs, looked up in wonder from their flower-gathering.

Angry Mr. Blipper

"Why, it's Bob Guess!" cried Bert, dropping his bunch of flowers, so excited was he. "It's Bob Guess!"

"So it is!" agreed Nan. "And he's crying."

There was no doubt of that: It was Bob Guess, the lad the Bobbsey twins had seen working at the merry-go-round engine the day of the Sunday school picnic. Bob came slowly along, sobbing hard.

"What's the matter, Bob?" asked Bert, who had taken a liking to the ragged chap. For the time being Mr. Bobbsey's missing coat and the lap robe were forgotten. "Why are you crying?"

"Can we help you?" asked Mrs. Bobbsey.

Bob Guess ceased sobbing and looked up. He seemed surprised to see the children and their parents.

"Oh, I—I didn't know anybody was here," he stammered.

"That's all right," said Mr. Bobbsey. "If there's anything we can do to help you— Where's Mr. Blipper, by the way? There is something I should like to ask him. Or perhaps you can tell me."

"Not now, Dick, not now," said Mrs. Bobbsey in a whisper, with a shake of her head at her husband. She knew what he wanted to ask—about his coat and the robe. "Not now; he is too miserable," she went on.

"Has anything happened?" asked Mr. Bobbsey, changing his first line of questions.

"Ye—yes," stammered Bob, not sobbing so hard now. "I—I've run away from Mr. Blipper!"

"You've run away!" echoed Nan.

Bob nodded his head vigorously to show that he meant "yes," and he went on:

"He treated me mean! There was a lot of hard work setting up the merry-go-round at the Bolton Fair, and I had more than my share. He wouldn't give me any money—he hardly gave me enough to eat. And I ran away. I'm not done running yet, only I'm so hungry I can't go very fast any more."

"You poor boy!" murmured Mrs. Bobbsey. "Is that why you cried—because you were hungry?"

"Yes—yes'm," murmured Bob Guess.

"Well, we have plenty to eat," said Mr. Bobbsey, with a kindly pat on the shoulder of the ragged boy. "Here, we'll give you a lunch, and then maybe you can tell me what I want to know. Where is Mr. Blipper?"

"He's back there at the merry-go-round. We had some trouble with the engine. But I guess he has it fixed by now. He's back at the fair grounds. It opens to-morrow. That is, he's there unless he has come chasing after me."

"Do you think he'd do that?" asked Bert. It was quite an exciting adventure, Bert thought, to run away and be chased by Mr. Blipper.

"Well, he said if I ever ran away he'd run after me and bring me back," answered Bob. "Anyhow, I've run away, but it isn't as much fun as I thought it'd be. Only I can't stand Mr. Blipper! He's too cross!"

"Poor boy!" murmured Mrs. Bobbsey again. "Get him something to eat, Dick. He must be very hungry!"

And Bob was, to judge by the manner in which he ate some of the Bobbsey's lunch. It was a good thing there was plenty. Having eaten all he seemed to care for and drinking two glasses of milk, Bob leaned back against a tree stump and said:

"Now can't I do something to pay you for my meal?"

"Do something to pay for it?" repeated Mrs. Bobbsey, wonderingly.

"Yes, Mr. Blipper says I've always got to work for my board. Sometimes he says I'm not worth my salt."

"Well, this time there is no need of doing anything for us," said Mr. Bobbsey. "You are welcome to what you have had to eat. But now what are you going to do?"

"I'm going to run away farther if I can," Bob Guess answered.

"Hum! I'm not so sure that we ought to let you, now that we know about you," went on the father of the Bobbsey twins. "Has this Mr. Blipper any claim on you?"

"He says he adopted me and can keep me until I'm twenty-one years old."

"He may be right. I don't know about that. It must be looked into. Anyhow, I don't feel like letting you run away, Bob," went on Mr. Bobbsey kindly. "I'd like to have a talk with Blipper on my own account, and I could ask him about you. Did you happen to see—"

But before Mr. Bobbsey could ask what he intended to—about his missing coat and the lap robe—a man from the garage where the automobile had been left to have the tire changed came across the field.

"It's a good thing you stopped when you did, Mr. Bobbsey," said the garage man.

"Why so?"

"Because if you had gone on a little farther one of the wheels of your car would have come off, and if you had been going fast, or down-hill, you might have had a bad accident. I found the break when I was putting on the tire, and I came over to ask if you wanted me to fix it."

"Yes, I suppose so. I'll come and have a look. We don't want to go on if there is any danger."

"There is danger. And it will take half a day to mend the break."

"Half a day!" said Mr. Bobbsey, as he followed the man, forgetting for the time all about Bob and Mr. Blipper. "That means we'll not get to Meadow Brook to-night. Is there a good hotel in town?"

"Yes, a very good one not far from my garage."

"Well then, in case we have to remain, we can stay at the hotel. But wait until I take a look at the broken wheel."

Mr. Bobbsey found that the garage man was right. The automobile was in need of repairs, and had the party gone on, without noticing the break, a bad accident might have happened.

"Oh, dear!" sighed Mrs. Bobbsey, when told of the news, "must we stay here all night?"

"Unless I hire another auto, or you and the children go on by train," said her husband. "I shall have to stay here to bring our car on."

"Oh, I don't want that! No, we'll stay at the hotel. But what about him?" she asked in a low voice, pointing to Bob Guess, who was talking to the twins.

"That's so. We can't turn him adrift," Mr. Bobbsey agreed. "Well, I'll get a room for him at the hotel. In the morning I can decide what to do. I don't like to send him back to Blipper. But if the man has adopted him he has a claim on the boy. We'll see what happens by morning."

Mrs. Bobbsey may have disliked to break the journey and stay at a strange hotel, but the Bobbsey twins thought it great fun. The hotel was a small country one, clean and neat, and the Bobbseys and Bob Guess were about the only guests there.

"I'm not fit to stop at a hotel," said the ragged boy.

"Oh, you're all right," said Mr. Bobbsey. "Perhaps I can get you some clothes here. If there isn't a store that sells them I may be able to get you a second-hand suit from the hotel keeper."

As it happened, there was no clothing store in the village of Montville, where the stop was made. But the hotel proprietor had some clothes of one of his sons who had gone to the city to work. Bob was given a partly worn but very good coat and trousers.

"He's a nice looking boy when he's dressed well," said Mrs. Bobbsey, as the lad discarded his old clothes.

"Yes," agreed her husband. "He has a good, honest face. And yet, when I think of my coat and the lap robe— But I'll wait until I see Blipper."

"Do you think you will see him?"

"Yes, I imagine he'll follow this boy. He's a hard worker, Bob is, and Blipper won't want to lose him. I shouldn't wonder but what he came on after Bob."

"How will he know where to find him?" asked Bert, who heard what his father and mother said.

"Oh, he can make inquiries along the way. But I'll do what I can for Bob."

Bert and Nan, with Flossie and Freddie, had good times at the country hotel. Their rooms were on a long corridor, and the twins raced up and down this, playing tag and other games. No one seemed to mind.

At supper Bob ate a good meal, but did not talk much. And every time the dining room door opened he looked around quickly, as if fearing to see Mr. Blipper come in.

In the evening Mr. Bobbsey went down to the garage to see how the men were progressing with the repairs to his car, for they had promised to work all night. Bert went with his father.

"I guess you'll be able to go on in the morning, Mr. Bobbsey," the garage man said.

"I hope so. My youngsters are anxious to get to Meadow Brook, and from there go to the Bolton County Fair."

"That's quite a fair. Lots of attractions I hear. A merry-go-round, a balloon, airships, and auto races. I'd go myself if I had time."

As Bert and his father reached the hotel a little later they heard loud talking coming from the sitting room where they had left Mrs. Bobbsey and the children. The voice of an angry man was saying:

"Well, I tell you I'm going to have that boy back! He ran away from me! I'm his legally appointed guardian, and I want him back! You come along with me, Bob Guess!"

Then Mrs. Bobbsey said firmly:

"Mr. Blipper, you shall not take this boy away until my husband comes back. Mr. Bobbsey wants to see you. You can't take Bob away like this. I won't let you. If necessary I'll call a policeman. You must wait until my husband comes back!"

"I'm not going to wait! I'm going to take that boy now!" cried the angry man, as Bert and his father hurried in.

The Big Swing

Mr. Bobbsey and Bert now looked on a rather sad scene in the hotel sitting room. On one side of the apartment stood Mr. Blipper, having hold of the coat collar of Bob Guess. And Bob was crying again.

On the other side of the room stood Mrs. Bobbsey with Nan, Flossie, and Freddie close to her. At one end of the room, looking in through the door, was the good-natured but easy-going proprietor of the hotel and some of the servants.

"What is going on here?" asked Mr. Bobbsey.

"I'm going away, if that's what you mean!" snapped out Mr. Blipper in angry tones. "I traced this runaway adopted son of mine here, and I'm taking him back with me. This lady says I can't!"

"I told him to wait until you came back," said Mrs. Bobbsey. "I didn't want him to take poor Bob away. I don't believe he has any right to take him."

"I don't know who you are!" spluttered the angry Mr. Blipper. "But you haven't any right to stop me."

"This lady is my wife," said Mr. Bobbsey, and he spoke in such a way that Mr. Blipper at once lost some of his bluster. "She has the same right that any one has to inquire into something he thinks is wrong."

"But this isn't wrong!" cried Mr. Blipper. "I have a right to this boy. I adopted him legally, I did! I gave him a name when he didn't have any before. Bob Guess I call him, 'cause I had to guess at his name. I took him out of an orphan asylum and give him a good home!"

"Home!" cried Bob Guess. "You didn't give me any *home*! You keep dragging me all over the country with that merry-go-round! I haven't any home except sleepin' in a truck."

"You were glad enough to come with me!" sneered Mr. Blipper.

"Anyway, I'm sick of it. That's why I ran away."

"Well, you're going to run back again!" said Mr. Blipper, grimly, as he gave the boy a shake.

"Wait a minute," said Mr. Bobbsey. "Have you a legal right to this boy?"

"That's what I have. I expected some such question would be asked of me, and I brought along my papers. There they are. You can look 'em over for yourself."

He tossed a long envelope containing papers to Mr. Bobbsey, and the latter looked at the documents.

"Don't let him take me back!" pleaded Bob Guess. "I don't like him!"

"I don't like you, when it comes to that!" sneered the angry man. "But I'm going to have you back! I have a right to you, and you've got to work for me."

"These papers seem to be all right," said Mr. Bobbsey, slowly. "He is your legal guardian, Bob. You had better go with him, and do as he says. But if he treats you cruelly let me know. I am going to the Bolton County Fair, and when I get there I'll keep my eye on you."

"Say, who are you, anyhow?" sneered Mr. Blipper.

"My name is Bobbsey," answered the children's father. "I live in Lakeport. I thought perhaps you might know my name."

"How should I know your name?"

"It was on some papers in my coat that disappeared from the Sunday school picnic grounds the day you had trouble with your engine near the grove."

Mr. Blipper looked first at Bob and then at Mr. Bobbsey.

"Say!" cried the merry-go-round owner, "maybe you think I know something about your coat."

"Maybe you do," answered Mr. Bobbsey, easily.

"And the lap robe!" whispered Bert.

"Hush, Bert!" warned his mother. "Leave this to Daddy!"

"Well, I don't know anything about your coat or a lap robe, either!" declared Mr. Blipper. "All I know is that Bob ran away from me, and now I'm going to run him back!"

There seemed no help for it. Mr. Bobbsey sadly shook his head when the twins and his wife pleaded with him to do something to save Bob.

"Those papers show the boy is adopted," he said. "I can do nothing. But we'll keep our eyes on him. We are going to the fair, and if Bob is not kindly treated I'll complain to the Children's Aid Society."

"You don't need to worry!" gruffly said Mr. Blipper. "I'll treat him as well as he deserves."

"Am I to keep these clothes?" asked Bob, as Mr. Blipper led him away.

"Of course," said Mr. Bobbsey. "I bought them for you."

"What's that? Who's been giving you clothes?" demanded Mr. Blipper.

"Don't you think he needed them?" inquired Mrs. Bobbsey, gently.

"Well—er—I was going to buy him a new suit after we took in some money at the Bolton Fair," sheepishly said Mr. Blipper. "I—I'm much obliged to you folks, though. Bob isn't a bad boy when he wants to be good. Come on now. I've a rig outside and we can get back to the fair grounds to-night if we hurry."

With a sad look at the friends who had been so kind to him, Bob followed his adopted father out of the room. He did not cry, but he seemed to want to.

"Good-by!" called the Bobbsey twins. "We'll see you at the fair!"

"Good-by!" echoed Bob Guess.

The Bobbsey twins wondered when they would see him again.

It might be thought that the excitement of the runaway boy who was caught again would keep Bert and Nan awake. Flossie and Freddie were too young to give the matter much attention. But though the older Bobbsey twins felt sorry for the lad, they had the idea that their father would make matters all right concerning him, and so they did not lie awake vainly worrying.

They slept soundly, the night passed quietly, and in the morning after an early breakfast the family were on their way again in the automobile which had been mended during the night.

"We'll soon be at Meadow Brook Farm, sha'n't we?" asked Freddie over and over again.

"Yes," his mother told him.

"And I'm going to milk a cow, I am!" announced Flossie.

"So'm I!" echoed Freddie. "I'm goin' milk two cows, I am!"

"I guess you mean you're going to see them milked!" laughed Nan. "Milking cows would be hard work even for Bert."

"Maybe I could milk a little teeny weeny cow," suggested Freddie.

"Well, we'll have some fun, anyhow!" said Nan.

And fun they did have! It started almost as soon as they reached the farm of their Uncle Daniel and Aunt Sarah.

"Say, I'm glad you came!" exclaimed Harry, as he greeted his four cousins while the older folks were talking among themselves. "I have something fine to show you."

"What?" asked Bert.

"A big swing! You ought to see it! It's out under the apple tree down by the brook!"

"Oh, I'm going to sail my boat in the brook!" cried Freddie, as soon as he heard the mention of water.

"An' I'll get Rosamond an' give her a ride on your boat!" cried Flossie. Rosamond was a small doll Flossie had brought along.

"All right," agreed Bert, seeing a chance for the smaller twins to play by themselves while he and Nan experimented with the swing. "You get your boat, Freddie, and you get your doll, Flossie, and we'll all go down to the brook and apple tree together."

"Be careful, now!" called Mrs. Bobbsey, as the children ran off.

"We will," they promised. And really they meant to, but you know how it often is—things happen that you can't help.

"There's the swing!" cried Harry, pointing to it dangling from the sturdy limb of the big apple tree. "Daddy put it up for me last week. I'm glad you came. We can have lots of fun in it."

"We want some swings!" cried Freddie.

"After a bit," promised Nan. "Sail your boat now, and give Rosamond a ride, Flossie, and you shall have some swings after that."

The water was more of an attraction for the smaller twins than was the swing, and thus Nan, Bert and Harry had it to themselves. While Flossie and Freddie played with the doll and the boat, the older children took turns seeing how high they could go. Then they would let the "old cat die," that is, stay in the swing, without trying to make it sway, until it came to a dead stop.

"I know what we can do!" cried Bert, when they were tired of swinging.

"What?" asked Harry.

"We can shinny up the rope like sailors. I can go 'way up to the limb."

Bert was a sturdy chap, and soon he was "shinnying," or climbing, up the rope like a human monkey. Then Harry did it, managing to reach the big limb, to which the rope was fastened, more quickly than had Bert.

"Now it's my turn!" exclaimed Nan, when the two boys were on the ground again.

"Pooh! Girls can't climb ropes!" declared Harry.

"Yes, I can, too! You watch!"

Nan was almost as strong as her brother. She caught hold of the rope, and managed to scramble up, though it was hard work.

"You can't do it!" laughed Harry, when, almost at the top, she paused for a moment.

"Yes, I can! I can! You just watch!"

Nan gave a wiggle, another scramble, and then, just as she managed to get one leg over the limb, she slipped.

"Oh! Oh!" she screamed. "I'm going to fall!"

But she did not fall. Instead, one foot caught in a loop of the rope, and there poor Nan hung, half way over the limb, one leg dangling down, and her hands clutching the rope. She could neither get up nor down! She was caught on the limb of the tree!

Down a Big Hole

For a few seconds Bert and Harry were so surprised at what had happened to Nan that they could do nothing but stand and stare up at her.

As for Nan, she also was surprised at the suddenness of her tumble when she was almost perched safely astride the limb to which the rope of the swing was tied. As she felt herself slipping she had clung with all her might, one hand and part of her arm over the branch, another hand grasping the rope, one leg partly up over the limb, and the other leg tangled in the rope.

This was what had caused the trouble—the leg getting caught and tangled in a loop of the rope. But for that, Nan could have swung this leg up over the limb and so have perched there in safety.

"Come on down!" cried Harry.

"Don't fall!" begged Bert. "Oh, Nan, be careful! Mother'll think I oughtn't to have let you climb up there!"

"You didn't—you didn't let—me!" panted Nan. "I did it myself!"

"Well, come on down!" begged Harry again.

"I—I can't!" half sobbed Nan, with a catch in her voice. "I—I'm stuck! Go get a ladder—get something to help me. I can't hold on much longer!"

"Shall we get the tennis net and let you fall into that?" asked Bert, starting toward the swing with half an idea that he could climb up the rope and loosen Nan.

"No, I don't want to fall!" cried his sister. "Get a ladder so I can climb down. Call daddy!"

"I'll call my father!" offered Harry. "He's got a long ladder!"

"Do something! Quick!" begged Nan desperately.

As Bert and Harry started to run toward the house to summon their fathers and mothers, Flossie and Freddie, tired of playing with the little boat in the brook, came up to the apple tree. Freddie saw Nan hanging there, some distance above the ground.

"Oh, Nan's doing circus tricks! Nan's doing circus tricks!" cried Freddie. "Look at her, Flossie. Nan's doing circus tricks an' I want to do 'em, too!"

"No, no, Freddie!" screamed Nan, as her little brother ran under the limb to which she was desperately clinging. "Go away! Don't stand under me this way! I might fall on you!"

"Oh, I'm going to get mother!" exclaimed Flossie. "She won't want you to fall, Nan!"

"Well, I—I can't hold on much longer!" sobbed Nan.

Though if she had let go her grasp on the tree limb she would probably not have fallen, for one foot was tangled in the swing rope. However, hanging by one leg high in the air would not have been very pleasant. Nan was not enough of a circus performer for that, though she and Bert had often done "stunts" on a trapeze in the back yard at home when they gave "shows."

However, help was on its way to Nan. The excited story told by Harry and Bert to the two Mr. Bobbseys started both men into action. They got a long ladder and, having run with it to the tree, placed it up against the limb. Then Mr. Richard Bobbsey climbed up, while his brother held steady the foot of the ladder on the ground.

"Why, Nan!" exclaimed her father, as he climbed up to set her free, "what in the world made you do this?"

"I—I don't know, Daddy! But Bert and Harry climbed up, and they did it all right. But when I went up something slipped, and I nearly fell, and I grabbed the rope and the branch, and there I was!"

"Well, it's a good thing you stuck here instead of falling down there," and Mr. Bobbsey looked to the ground below. "You're all right now. Don't cry."

But Nan could not help crying a little, though she was glad she could feel her father's arms about her. Mr. Bobbsey soon loosened the little girl's leg from the loop of the rope, and then he carried her down the ladder.

"You're just like a fireman, aren't you, Daddy?" cried Freddie, as his father set Nan on the ground.

"Well, a little, yes," admitted Mr. Bobbsey, with a laugh. "But better not any more of you try those firemen tricks," he warned the children as the ladder was taken down.

"I'll have to put the swing away if you climb the rope any more," threatened Uncle Daniel.

"We won't shinny up it any more," promised Bert and Harry, and their fathers knew that if the boys did not do it Nan would not.

"I guess we've had enough swinging," said Bert. "Let's play something else, Harry. Got any new games?"

"We can go down to the pond and fish."

"Oh, I love to fish!" exclaimed Nan. "What kind of fish can you catch in the pond, Harry?"

"Bullfrogs, mostly."

"They aren't fish," laughed Nan.

"Well, it's just as much fun," went on the country boy.

"I guess I'd better go help mother unpack the trunks," Nan said, for she saw the expressman drive up with two trunks that had been sent on ahead. "Mother will want me to help her get the things out so we can go to the Bolton County Fair to-morrow. You're coming, aren't you, Harry?"

"Sure! It'll be great. But now we'll go fishing for bullfrogs. Come on, Bert!"

"I want to fish!" begged Freddie, hearing this magic word.

"No, you and Flossie come with me," directed Nan, knowing that the two boys would not have much fun if they had to watch the small children and keep them from tumbling into the pond.

"Don't want to come with you!" pouted Flossie. "We wants to go fishing!"

"How would you and Freddie like to go after eggs?" asked Nan, as she saw her brother and Harry making signals to her for her to do her best to keep Flossie and Freddie from following. "Wouldn't you like to gather eggs?"

"Where do you get the eggs?" asked Freddie, who had forgotten.

"In the barn. We'll take the eggs out of the nests, and you and Flossie can carry the eggs in a little basket to Aunt Bobbsey."

"Oh, yes!" cried Flossie. "I want to do that!"

"So do I!" added Freddie. Anything Flossie wanted to do he generally did also.

"All right," said Nan, waving to Bert and Harry to hurry away before the small twins changed their minds. "Come with me, and after I help mother unpack the trunk we'll go and get the eggs."

As it happened, however, Mrs. Bobbsey did not need Nan's help. Aunt Sarah said she would aid in getting the things out of the trunks, so Nan was allowed to go with Flossie and Freddie to the barn to gather eggs.

What fun it was to climb over the sweet hay, sliding down little hills of it and landing on the barn floor, where more hay made a place like a cushion!

What fun it was to look in at the horses chewing their fodder! And when the children poked their heads in the horses stopped eating, to turn around and look to see who was watching them.

"Oh, I've found some eggs!" suddenly cried Flossie, as she spied some of the white objects in a nest in the hay.

"Pick them up carefully," advised Nan. "Eggs break very easily."

"I want to help pick up the eggs!" cried Freddie, hurrying over to his little sister's side.

"No, you go find a nest of your own!" exclaimed Flossie. "These are my eggs!"

"There are plenty of nests," said Nan. "You ought each to find two or three. Come on, Freddie, we'll look for a nest for you. Be careful of those eggs, Flossie! I guess I'd better help you pick them up and put them in a basket while Freddie looks for another nest."

So while Nan stayed with Flossie, Freddie started off by himself to look for another nest. And as Nan discovered a second nest not far from where Flossie had found the first one, it took the sisters some time to pick up all the eggs.

This gave Freddie more time to himself, and he saw a ladder leading into the upper part of the barn where most of the hay was stored.

"I guess maybe I'll find eggs up there," he said.

He climbed the ladder, going slowly and carefully, and soon found himself up in the haymow. It was rather dark there, but when he had been in the place a little while Freddie could see better.

"I guess hens come up here to lay 'cause it's nice and quiet. Now I must find some nests and eggs."

He walked about over the slippery hay, peering here and there for a cluster of white eggs. Suddenly Freddie felt himself sliding down. Faster and faster he went, feet first, and before he knew it he had slid down into a big hole together with a lot of hay.

"Nan! Nan!" he cried. "Come an' get me! I'm down in a hole!"

The County Fair

Just as Nan and Flossie finished putting the last of the eggs into their basket they heard Freddie's cries for help. Surprised and a little frightened, they ran out of that part of the barn where Flossie had found the first nest and Nan the second.

"Freddie! Freddie!" cried Nan. "Where are you, Freddie?"

"Down in a hole!" came the muffled answer.

"What hole?" Nan wanted to know. "Tell me where the hole is so I can come and get you out. What hole, Freddie?"

"Maybe it's a dark hole," suggested Flossie. "You 'member the verse: 'Charcoal! Charcoal! Put me in a dark hole.' Maybe Freddie is in a dark hole."

"Yes, it is dark!" again sounded the muffled voice of the little boy. "I can hear you, Nan, but I can't see you. Get me out of the dark hole!"

Nan was puzzled. She, too, could hear Freddie calling, but she could not see him. There were so many nooks and corners in the old barn that it was not strange Freddie was not easily found. It was a great place for playing hide and go seek, so many dark spots were there in which to crouch, and the seeker might be right alongside of you and not spy you.

"How did you get in the hole, Freddie?" asked Nan, knowing that talking and listening to Freddie's answers was the best way to find out where he was.

"I was looking for a nest," he said, his voice still muffled and far away, "and I slipped on some hay and went down the hole. There's a lot of hay in the hole with me now, and I'm stuck. I'm about half way down in the hole, Nan."

Then Nan began to understand what had taken place. She remembered that once something like this had happened to her.

"Are you sliding down or standing still, Freddie?" she called to her brother.

"I was sliding, but I'm standing still now," he answered. "I'm stuck fast in a lot of hay."

"Well, wiggle as hard as you can," advised Nan. "I know where you are. You're in one of the chutes, or wooden tubes, that Uncle Daniel shoves hay down from the top floor of the barn to the lower floor. You stepped into a hay chute and you're stuck half way down. Wiggle, and you'll slide down the rest of the way and you'll be out."

So Freddie wiggled as hard as he could and, surely enough, he felt himself again sliding down. He was not hurt, for there was soft hay on all sides of him. But it tickled, and it scratched the back of his neck, as well as his hands and face.

Some of the hay dust got up his nose, too, and made him want to sneeze. He gave one little sneeze—making a queer sound cooped up as he was—and then he cried:

"Oh, I'm stuck again, Nan! I started sliding and now I'm stuck again!"

"Wiggle some more," advised his sister.

She had set down the basket of eggs and was looking toward a dark side of the barn where she could see the lower ends of several wooden chutes. Some were for oats and others for hay. She did not know just which wooden chute Freddie would slide down. The chutes did not come all the way to the floor, there being room under each one to set a box or bushel basket.

"Wiggle some more, Freddie!" again advised Nan.

"I will!" came the answer. "I'll wiggle hard and I'll—Oh—kerchoo!"

That was Freddie sneezing, and he sneezed so hard that it did more good than his wiggling, for it sent him sliding down with a mass of hay to the bottom of the chute.

"Here I am!" he cried, and with a thump he landed on the barn floor, so wrapped and tangled in a clump of hay that he was not in the least hurt. "I'm all—kerchoo—right—kerchoo—Nan!" he said, talking and sneezing at the same time.

"Well, I'm glad we found you, anyhow!" laughed his sister. "How did it happen?"

"Oh, it just happened," was all Freddie could say. "I was looking for eggs, and I slipped. I'm glad I didn't slip in a hen's nest, else I'd 'a' broken a lot of eggs."

"I'm glad of that, too," agreed Nan. "Well, Flossie and I are 'way ahead of you. We have found two nests!"

"I'm going to find one myself!" declared Freddie, and a little later he did. This nest had many eggs in it, for it was used by several hens in turn, so that now the basket was half filled.

Then, by searching about, the children found more nests and eggs until the basket was quite full. Now arose a dispute between Flossie and Freddie, for each one wanted to carry the basket. Nan was afraid either of the little twins might stumble and fall, thereby breaking the eggs.

"I know what we'll do," Nan said, making up a little plan, as she often had to do to get Freddie and Flossie into a new way of thinking. "We'll play hide and go seek. I'll go on ahead and hide, and whoever finds me can carry the basket a little way."

"Oh, that'll be fun!" cried Freddie. "Come on, Flossie! Blind your eyes."

"Don't come until I get ready!" said Nan.

The children promised they would not. Carefully they closed their eyes, covering them with their hands. Nan hurried away, walking softly so the twins could not guess which way she was going. And she picked out a hiding place close to the house, right at the foot of the steps, in fact.

"Whichever one finds me won't have very far to carry the eggs, and they won't be so likely to drop them," thought Nan, as she crouched down behind the rain-water barrel.

"Coop!" cried Nan, this being a signal that she was hidden.

"Ready or not we're coming!" shouted Freddie. He and his sister opened their eyes and began running about, eagerly searching. It was some little time before they found Nan behind the barrel, and Flossie spied her first.

"I see you! I see you!" laughed the delighted little girl, and she was so excited over finding Nan that she never realized she had only a few steps to carry the basket of eggs.

Flossie covered those few steps safely, and the eggs were put away in the closet by Aunt Sarah, later to be made into puddings and cakes for the Bobbsey twins.

"When are we going to the Bolton County Fair?" asked Bert that evening after supper, when he and Harry were resting after their sport in catching bullfrogs.

"And I'm going to ride on a lion!" declared Freddie.

"We might go over to the fair to-morrow," said Mr. Bobbsey. "Do you folks want to go?" he asked his brother and Aunt Sarah.

"I don't believe I'll have time," answered Mr. Bobbsey's brother.

"Nor I," said Aunt Sarah. "I have a lot of cooking to do."

"Then I'm going to stay at home and help you," offered the mother of the Bobbsey twins.

"Oh, can't we go to the fair?" wailed Flossie and Freddie, almost ready to cry.

"Of course you may go!" replied Mother Bobbsey. "I was going to say that daddy could take you children—Harry may go, may he not?" she asked his mother.

"Oh, yes."

"Hurray!" cried Harry, and Bert and Nan echoed his cry of joy.

So it was arranged that Mr. Bobbsey would take the children to the Bolton County Fair, there to see the many wonderful things of which they had dreamed for days and nights.

The Bolton County Fair was one of the largest in that part of the state. Every year it was held, and farmers from many miles away brought their largest pumpkins and squashes, and their longest ears of corn, hoping to win prizes with them. The farmers' wives brought samples of their needlework, such as bedquilts, lace or embroidery, and samples of their cooking and preserving. The farm boys and girls made things or raised something to exhibit at the fair.

Besides this there were new kinds of machinery for the farmers to look at, such as windmills and plows and electrical appliances to be used on the farms. Men who raised horses and cattle took their best specimens to the fair to show them for prizes.

Then there were to be automobile races and horse races, and there were many amusements from the big merry-go-round to the little tents and booths where one could throw baseballs at dolls or toss rings over canes. There were also booths and tents where candy, ice-cream, lemonade and cider were sold, as well as places to eat.

"Oh, it's wonderful!" cried Nan, as she and her brothers, her sister, Harry and her father got out of their automobile and walked through the big gates into the fair grounds. "Don't you like it, Bert?"

"Sure! It's fine!"

"Let's go over and look at the airship," proposed Harry.

"And the balloon," added Bert. "Do you s'pose I could go up in the balloon?" he asked his father.

"No, I don't suppose you could—I wouldn't like you to," said Mr. Bobbsey.

"But why, Dad? The balloon is fast to the ground. It can't get away!"

"I'm not so sure about that. I don't want you to go up. You'll have plenty of other fun."

"I wanted to go up in the balloon," and Bert sighed in disappointment.

"We'll go look at it, anyhow," suggested Harry.

"I want a ride on a lion!" insisted Freddie.

"So do I!" added Flossie.

"All right, I'll take you children to the merry-go-round," said Mr. Bobbsey. "You come there and meet us after you finish looking at the balloon and the airship," he said to Bert and Harry.

"I'll stay with you, Daddy," said Nan. "I want a ride on the merry-go-round, too," and she laughed.

They could hear the music of the "carrousel," as a merry-go-round is sometimes called.

"Come on!" urged Flossie and Freddie, tugging at their father's hands.

He led them over to the crowd that surrounded the machine on which a whirling ride could be had for five cents.

"This way! This way for the merry-go-round!" cried a boy's voice. "Only five cents a ride! Get your tickets and take a ride! On an elephant or a tiger!"

"I want a lion!" cried Freddie.

"All right! This way for your lions!" cried the voice.

Mr. Bobbsey, pushing his way through the crowd with the children, saw Bob Guess on the merry-go-round. The boy was helping children to their seats on the wooden animals, strapping them safely so they would be ready when the machinery started. The organ kept on playing all the while.

"Hello, Bob!" called Nan, as she climbed up on a wooden horse, while Flossie and Freddie, with their father, looked for lions.

The strange boy glanced up in some surprise. But when he saw Nan a smile came over his rather sad face.

"Oh, hello!" he said. "How did you get here?"

"We came just now in my father's auto. Do you run the merry-go-round?"

"I help when Mr. Blipper isn't here. I take up the tickets after she starts. Have you got your tickets?"

"Yes, daddy bought them. My little brother and sister want to ride on lions."

"There's a pair right behind you," said Bob Guess.

Nan turned and saw her father just finishing the strapping up of Flossie and Freddie each on a big wooden lion. The small twins were smiling with delight.

"Gid-dap!" called Flossie to her lion.

"You shouldn't say 'gid-dap' to a lion," objected Freddie.

"What should you say?" asked Flossie, turning to look at her brother.

"You ought to say—now—er—'Scat!'"

"That's what you say to a cat!" declared Flossie.

"Well, then say 'Boo!' I guess that's what you say to a lion," went on Freddie. "Say 'Boo!'"

The little girl looked doubtful.

"All right. Boo!" cried Flossie, after a moment.

It was not quite time, however, for the merry-go-round to start. Mr. Bobbsey made his way along the platform to Bob, who stood near Nan.

"Where is Mr. Blipper?" asked Mr. Bobbsey. "I want to see him."

"He's away to-day, Mr. Bobbsey," was the answer.

"Away! Oh, I am sorry," was the reply of the Bobbsey twins' father.

"This is his day off," went on the lad.

"Will he be here to-morrow?"

"Yes, sir. But look out now, she's going to start!"

On the Track

Creaking and squeaking as it slowly started, the merry-go-round began to go faster and faster until it was whirling rapidly, the music of the organ mingling with the shouts of the delighted children.

Seeing that Flossie and Freddie were all right, being strapped to their wooden lions, and that Nan could look after herself, Mr. Bobbsey took a seat in one of the gilded cars that were provided for older persons who did not like to sit astride a wooden animal. He watched Bob Guess making his way around the carrousel collecting the tickets. The boy seemed bright and very business like.

"He's a good lad," thought Mr. Bobbsey. "I wish a better man than Mr. Blipper had charge of him. I must look into this matter."

At one place on the outside of the merry-go-round was a post with an arm extending down from it. Into this arm, which was hollow, a boy dropped iron rings, with, now and then, a brass one among them. Those whirling about on the carrousel could reach up and pull a ring from the arm, if they were quick and skillful enough.

"Get the brass ring and have a free ride!" sang out the boy dropping the black, iron rings into the hollow arm. There were, a great many iron rings, but only a few brass ones. Of course, every one wanted to get the brass ring, but this went by luck as much as by skill.

Flossie and Freddie were too small to reach over and try for any of the rings. But Nan, like the older boys and girls and some of the grown folks, had no trouble in catching rings.

"Get the brass ring, and have an extra ride!" cried the boy in charge.

"I wish I could!" thought Nan.

Once she almost got it. She saw the brass ring gleaming at the end of the arm. A boy two horses ahead of her made a grab for it and missed. So did the girl directly in front of Nan. When Nan reached for the ring she did not put out her arm far enough, and she, too, missed it. A girl riding on a camel behind Nan got it.

"Oh, dear!" sighed Nan.

"Never mind," said a voice at her side, and she saw Bob Guess. "Here's a brass ring for you. Take it and have the next ride free!"

"Oh, will that be right?" asked Nan.

"Sure it will! I'm in charge of taking the tickets when Blipper is away. Some one grabbed this ring and dropped it. I picked it up. It's good for a ride. Take it. I don't know who dropped it or I'd give it to 'em. You take it!"

And Nan did. It was not to be dreamed of that Flossie and Freddie would be content with one ride. They had to stay on for the second. Mr. Bobbsey got off to buy more tickets.

"I don't need a ticket!" Nan called to him. "I have the brass ring, Daddy!"

"Oh, you were very lucky!"

"Bob gave it to me," she explained, telling how it came about.

"Well, I suppose it is all right to take it," her father said. "Bob knows what he is doing."

"But I want to get a brass ring my own self," Nan said. And she did, though not on the next trip. Her father had to buy her a ticket for that.

Then came the final ride, for though Flossie and Freddie would have remained and ridden all day, their father knew this was not good for them. And it was on the last ride that Nan got her brass ring.

"Oh, now I can ride again!" she gayly cried.

"Not now," her father told her. "If you ride, Flossie and Freddie will want to, and I'm afraid they'll be ill."

"But what shall I do with the ring?" asked Nan, slipping down off the wooden horse and holding up the brass ring.

"It'll be good to-morrow," said Bob Guess. "You can keep it, or I'll save it here for you."

"I guess you'd better keep it, Bob," said Nan, with a laugh. "I might lose it."

"I'll save it for you," promised Bob. "I'll look for you to-morrow. Get your tickets—your tickets for the merry-go-round!" he cried, as a new crowd surged up to get on.

"May we have some pop corn?" asked Freddie, when told there were to be no more rides that day.

"And ice-cream?" added Flossie.

"Dear me!" laughed Mr. Bobbsey, "I don't know which will be worse for you. Let's look about a bit."

"I'm thirsty!" announced Flossie.

"Well, we'll have some lemonade—that will be good for all of us, I think," suggested Mr. Bobbsey. Bert and Harry, coming back just then from having been to look at the balloon, were taken to the lemonade stand with the others.

If I were to tell you all the things the Bobbsey twins saw at the County Fair and all they did, it would take a larger book than this to hold it all. So I can only tell you a few of the many things that happened.

After drinking the lemonade the children hardly knew at what to look next, there were so many things to see. Presently Mr. Bobbsey said:

"You have been among a lot of wooden animals on the merry-go-round, suppose we go see some real, live animals?"

"Oh, yes!" cried Nan.

"Let's go to see the race horses," suggested Bert.

"And I want to see cows and pigs!" announced Freddie.

"And sheeps! I want to see sheeps!" exclaimed Flossie.

"They're on the way to the racing horse stables," explained Harry. "All the live stock is together."

There was a race track at the fair grounds and some races had been run off before the Bobbseys arrived. More were to take place soon.

Mr. Bobbsey and the other children were so interested in looking at the prize cattle, at great hogs, some weighing nearly a thousand pounds, and at bulls weighing more than this, that they did not notice the absence of Freddie Bobbsey. That little chap, however, had slipped away and, before he knew it, he was in the stable with the race horses.

As many of the stablemen were outside with their animals, some bringing their steeds back from the track and others taking racers over to have a part in the next contest, there were not many persons in the stable when Freddie wandered there.

"Oh, what a nice lot of horses!" he exclaimed, and indeed the racers were among the best of their kind. "I like horses!" went on Freddie.

One beautiful animal leaned out of its stall and rubbed a velvet nose on Freddie's shoulder.

"You like me, don't you, horsie?" asked the little chap. The horse whinnied, which might mean anything, but Freddie took it for "yes."

"I guess maybe you'd like to have me get on your back," he said. "I got on one of Uncle Dan's horses once. I know how to ride."

The horse was in a large box stall, and the door was not hard to open. In walked Freddie, and, by standing up on a keg which was in the stall, he managed to scramble up on the back of the horse. To keep from sliding off, though, Freddie had to clasp his arms around the neck of the animal.

Whether the horse took this for a signal to move along, or whether it just "happened," I don't know. But the horse walked out of the stall, across the grass of the paddock, and, as the big gate happened to be open, he walked right out on the race track with Freddie clinging to his neck.

In the Cornfield

Just about this time a race was going to be run. There were a number of horses, with jockey lads on their backs, waiting for the signal to begin their fast pace around the track. Up in the booth, where the judges and the starter were standing to give the signal, everything was in readiness. The people around the race track were all excited, for they wanted to see which horse would win.

And then, just as the starter gave the word, and the jockey boys on their horses' backs called to their steeds to run fast, out on the track walked the horse to whose neck Freddie was clinging!

At first the little fellow had been so startled when the animal to whose back he had scrambled walked out of the barn with him that he had not known what to do. He just clung there.

But, finding that the horse was very gentle and did not try to reach back and bite his legs, Freddie began rather to like it.

"Go 'long, nice horsie! Go 'long!" called Freddie, and he clapped his heels against the sides of the animal.

The horse went along all right—fairly out on to the race track, and just as the race was starting!

"Here! Where you going?"

"Come back with that horse!"

"Look out! Stop him, somebody! That boy will be hurt!"

These were only a few of the many cries that rose from the grandstand and the space in front of it when the people saw Freddie right in the path of the rushing horses.

"Ring that bell!" cried one of the judges to the starter.

The starter pulled the cord of the big gong which is rung to bring the horses back if they have not made an even start, as very often happens.

Clang! went the gong. The jockeys on the backs of the horses knew what the ringing of the bell meant. Some of them had begun to guide their horses so as not to run into Freddie and his mount, but there were so many racers that one or two of them might have bumped into the little fellow. But when the jockeys heard the ringing of the bell they knew it was a false start and they pulled in their steeds and some turned back.

But now something else happened. While the horse Freddie had climbed up on was kind and gentle, yet he was a race horse. And as soon as he found himself out on the track he must have thought he had been ridden there to take part in a race.

At any rate, before Freddie could stop him, even if the little Bobbsey lad had been able to do this, the horse began to trot around the track. Perhaps he thought the ringing of the bell meant for him to start.

So away he ran, going faster and faster with poor Freddie bobbing up and down, but still clinging to the animal's neck. It was all Freddie could do, as there was no saddle horn to grasp.

"Whoa! Whoa!" begged the little chap. "Nice horsie! Whoa now!"

It was not so much fun as Freddie had at first thought to take a ride in this way. At the beginning he had an idea that he might some day be a jockey and wear a gayly colored silk blouse. But he never imagined race horses went so fast.

"Whoa! Whoa!" cried Freddie again. But his horse did not stop. Indeed, it only went faster.

"Somebody get after that boy!" yelled the starter, leaning from the judges' stand. "He'll be hurt if you don't get him!"

"I'll get him!" offered one of the jockeys. He called to his horse and was soon speeding around the track after Freddie. And now the horse on whose back the little Bobbsey boy was seated, hearing another steed coming after him, began to think it was a race in real earnest, and he commenced to go faster. All the "whoa" shouts Freddie uttered were of no use.

"Go on, Tomato! Go on!" cried the jockey to his horse. "Go on, Tomato!" Tomato was the name of his animal.

The shouts and the screams of the crowd attracted the attention of Mr. Bobbsey and the other children as they came from the animal tent. And as Mr. Bobbsey neared the race track he had a glimpse of his little son clinging to a horse and riding very fast, while a jockey on another horse chased him.

"Oh, look! Freddie's in a race!" cried Flossie! "Oh, maybe Freddie will win!"

"My goodness! how did this happen?" cried Mr. Bobbsey.

"Will he be hurt?" gasped Nan.

But just then, to the great relief of the Bobbsey family, the jockey managed to come up alongside of Freddie's galloping horse. The jockey reached over with one hand, caught Freddie by the seat of his little trousers, and fairly lifted him off the back of the now excited horse.

Then, placing Freddie on the saddle in front of him, the jockey turned his horse about and rode slowly back to the stand. Some of the stablemen then ran out and caught the other horse.

"Why, Freddie! what in the world were you trying to do?" asked his father, when the little boy was placed in his arms.

"I—I just wanted a ride," Freddie explained. "I got tired of ridin' on wooden lions. I wanted a live horse."

"Well, he picked a lively one all right!" laughed a man in the crowd. "That horse he rode has won every race, so far."

"You must never do such a thing again, Freddie," his father told him, when the excitement had died down and the racing was once more started. "Never again."

"No, I won't," Freddie promised. "But when I grow up I'm goin' to ride horses, I am!"

"That will be a good while yet," laughed Bert.

"I'm glad your mother wasn't here," said Mr. Bobbsey. "She would have almost fainted, I'm sure, if she had seen you out on the race track like a regular jockey."

"Did I look like a jockey?" Freddie asked, eagerly.

"Well, not exactly," Bert said. "You didn't have any silk blouse on."

"I'll get Dinah to make me one when I go home," Freddie declared. "I'll have a red one, I guess, and then if I get tired of ridin' horses I can be a fireman."

"Well, I think we've had excitement enough for one day," remarked Mr. Bobbsey. "We'll have something to eat, look around a little more, and then go home."

"But we can come back again, can't we?" asked Bert. "I haven't seen the balloon go up yet."

"Yes, we want to see that," added Harry.

"I'll bring you to the fair again to-morrow or next day," promised Mr. Bobbsey. "I want to come back myself. I've met a number of men to-day I'd like to talk with further. Then I'd like to have a talk with that Mr. Blipper."

That night, at Meadow Brook Farm, Mr. Bobbsey and his wife, after the children had gone to bed, talked over the strange disappearance of Mr. Bobbsey's coat and the auto lap robe.

"I'm sure that Blipper knows something about them," said Mrs. Bobbsey. "Or perhaps that strange Bob Guess—what an odd name."

"It is an odd name," agreed Mr. Bobbsey, "But it fits, for they don't know what his real name is—at least he says he doesn't. But I don't believe Bob had anything to do with the taking of my coat and the robe. I'd like to find out more about the boy. He seems bright, and I feel sorry for him. I must see that man, Blipper, and have a talk with him."

"Wasn't he at his merry-go-round to-day?" asked Mrs. Bobbsey.

"No, he had gone off somewhere. But I am going to the fair again with the children, and I'll get at Blipper sooner or later."

"Well, if you go to the fair again, please keep an eye on Freddie!" begged the mother of the Bobbsey twins. "He's a little tyke when it comes to slipping away and doing strange things."

"Yes, he is," agreed her husband. But the next day was to prove that Flossie could also "slip away," when there was a chance.

The Bobbsey twins, with Harry, were out in the cornfield gathering ears of corn to feed to the hogs and chickens. The corn had been cut and stacked into piles called "shocks," and it was from the stalks in these shocks that the ears of yellow corn were broken off and placed in baskets to be taken to the house.

"Let's play hide and go seek for a while," suggested Nan to her brother and Harry. "Flossie and Freddie are over there by themselves, shelling corn." The smaller twins had been given a little basket, and they were now busy breaking off kernels of corn from some small ears, and dropping the corn into their basket.

"For the chickies," Flossie had explained.

So while the smaller twins were thus "kept out of mischief," as Nan said, she, with Bert and Harry, began a game of hide and go seek. It was lots of fun, dodging in and out among the tall corn shocks, which rose above the children's heads. The game went on for some time, until even Bert and Harry said they were tired.

"Well, we'll take the corn up to the house," announced Nan. "Come, Flossie and Freddie," she called. Freddie came up, carrying the basket of shelled corn, but Flossie was not with him.

"Where's your sister?" asked Harry.

"Who, Flossie? Oh, she went away. She said she was going home," Freddie answered. "She went home a good while ago!"

"Went home!" echoed Nan, with a gasping breath. "Why, she never could find the way all by herself. Oh, maybe she's lost!"

Freddie and the Pumpkin

The cornfield where the Bobbsey twins and Harry had gone to work and play was a long distance from the farmhouse. Nan knew this, and that is why she was frightened when Freddie said that Flossie had "gone home."

"Maybe she could find her way," said Bert.

"She's a smart little girl," added Harry. "I wish I had a sister like her."

"How long ago did she leave you, Freddie?" asked Nan.

"Oh, 'bout maybe three four hours," answered the little boy.

"We haven't been here an hour!" exclaimed Bert.

"Well, maybe it was minutes, then," admitted Freddie. He did not have a very good idea of time, you see.

"If it was only a little while ago she can't have gone very far," said Nan. "Flossie! Flossie!" she called. "Where are you?"

But there was no answer. Bert and Harry then took up the call, as they had louder voices than had Nan, and even Freddie added his shout, but it was of no use. Flossie did not answer.

"I guess she's too far away," Harry stated.

"We'd better hurry after her!" said Bert.

"Oh, come on!" cried Nan, half sobbing. "Mother told me to keep good watch over her, and I didn't! I shouldn't have played hide and go seek!"

"It wasn't your fault!" her brother consoled her. "It was as much mine as yours. But we'll find Flossie all right. I guess she's home by this time."

But when they had hurried to the farmhouse there was no sign of the little girl. Mrs. Bobbsey became much frightened when told what had happened.

"Is there any water she could fall into?" she asked Aunt Sarah.

"No, not even a duck pond near the cornfield. She's all right, I'm sure," said the other Mrs. Bobbsey. "We'll go back to the cornfield and find her hiding, I feel certain."

"But she wasn't playing hide and go seek," declared Nan. "She wouldn't hide from us."

"You can't tell," said Aunt Sarah, so cheerfully that the others took heart. Back they hurried to the field where the big shocks of dried cornstalks stood. The two Mr. Bobbseys also went along to help in the search.

"Now show us where you and Flossie were playing at shell the corn," said the mother of the twins.

"Right here," Freddie stated, and he pointed to some of the yellow kernels on the ground.

The father of the Bobbsey twins stooped down and looked at the soft earth. He soon found what he was looking for—the tiny footprints of his little girl.

"She went over this way," he said. "Come on, we'll pretend we are hunters on the trail. We'll soon find Flossie."

"Oh, this is fun!" laughed Freddie. But it was not exactly fun for the others. Even Nan and Bert were worried.

The footprints of Flossie wandered off among the shocks of corn, and in a few moments they stopped at a place where two or three shocks had been piled together, making a large heap.

And then, before any one could say a word, from behind this pile of cornstalks a sleepy voice called, asking:

"Where are you, Freddie?"

"There she is! That's Flossie!" cried Bert.

He and his mother made a dash around the big shock and there, lying with her little cloak wrapped around her, was Flossie, nestled amid the corn husks, curled up and just awakening from a nap.

"Oh, Flossie! why did you run away?" asked her mother, clasping her little daughter in her arms.

"I didn't runned away, I walked!" declared Flossie, rubbing her eyes. "What you all lookin' at me for?" she wanted to know. "Was I a bad girl, Mother?"

"Not exactly bad, but you frightened us," her father said. "However, we're glad we have found you."

Flossie had just wandered away by herself, unnoticed by Bert, Nan, or Harry, and, growing tired and sleepy, had nestled in the corn to take a nap. Freddie had been so busy shelling corn that he did not notice which way his little sister went.

But everything was all right now, and the happy families went back to the farmhouse, the smaller twins being allowed to feed some of their corn to the chickens.

True to his promise, Mr. Richard Bobbsey took his children to the Bolton County Fair the next day, his wife going with him this time. Of course Harry also went along, for it would not have been polite to leave him at home. As for Uncle Daniel and Aunt Sarah, they said they would go to the fair another day.

"Will you ask Mr. Blipper about your coat and the missing robe?" asked Mrs. Bobbsey, on the way to the fair grounds.

"Yes. And I'll ask him about Bob Guess, also," her husband answered. "There is something strange about that boy."

The Bobbsey twins and Harry were talking among themselves, while Nan also looked after Flossie and Freddie.

"They're going to put the big balloon up to-day," said Harry.

"They are if the wind doesn't blow too much," Bert agreed. "And I'm afraid it's blowing too hard. Do you think the wind is blowing too much for them to send the big balloon up?" he anxiously asked his father.

Mr. Bobbsey looked at the sky.

"To my mind," he said, "I think there is going to be a storm. I'm afraid the wind will keep on blowing harder all day. Of course I don't know how strong a wind it takes to keep a balloon man from going up, but I should say there would be danger in going up to-day."

"Oh, dear!" exclaimed Bert. "I wanted to see the man go up in the balloon!"

"So did I!" added Harry. "But maybe the wind will die out."

However, it did not, and it was still blowing rather hard when the fair grounds were reached.

"Never mind," said Mrs. Bobbsey, when she saw how disappointed Harry and Bert seemed to feel. "If the balloon doesn't go up to-day it will to-morrow, and we can come again. There are plenty of other things to look at besides balloons."

"I'd like to go to see some of the big vegetables and the fruits, and look at the patchwork quilts and the lace," said Nan.

"Very well," agreed her father. "We'll go there first, and maybe by that time the wind will have died down. But I hardly think so."

Truth to tell Bert and Harry did not care much for the big pumpkins, squashes, and other vegetables. And they hardly looked at the fancy work in which Nan and her mother took an interest.

"Oh, wouldn't this make a dandy jack-o'-lantern!" cried Freddie, as he crawled under a railing around a platform, on which were many large vegetables. "Look what a big pumpkin!"

"Freddie, you mustn't go in there," called his mother. "Come out. Don't touch that big pumpkin."

But it was too late! Freddie was already on the wooden platform, and he was rolling the pumpkin. It was almost perfectly round, and the little fellow could easily move it.

"Come away!" called Mr. Bobbsey, adding his voice to that of his wife.

"I want to see if I can lift this pumpkin!" exclaimed Freddie.

And then, suddenly, the big pumpkin rolled off the platform, toward the back of the tent.

"Get it, Freddie! Get it!" cried Bert, for he knew the pumpkin was on exhibition in order to take a prize, if possible. It would be too bad if anything happened to it.

Freddie made a dive for the big, yellow vegetable, but, as it happened, the tent stood on the top of a hill. And as the pumpkin rolled off the platform it slipped under the tent and began going down the grassy hill outside.

"Whoa! Whoa!" called Freddie, as he had called to the race horse that had walked out on the track with him. "Whoa, pumpkin!"

But the pumpkin kept on rolling! The little chap made a dive for it, missed it by a few inches, and then, falling over, he, too, rolled out under the tent and down the hill.

Freddie was not quite so round as a pumpkin, but he managed to get a good start, and rolled over and over. And as his father, mother, and the others hurried out of the tent they saw Freddie and the big yellow vegetable tumbling down the hill together.

"Oh, look! Look!" cried a little girl. "A boy and a pumpkin are having a race! Oh, look! How funny! A boy and a pumpkin are having a race!"

Up in a Balloon

The pumpkin won the race. I suppose you had already guessed that it would. For the pumpkin, being almost perfectly round, could roll down the hill faster than Freddie could.

So the pumpkin was the first to reach the bottom of the little grassy hill on which stood the tent where the prize fruits and vegetables were on exhibition. And Freddie came tumbling after, like Jack and Jill, you know.

And I believe it is a good thing the pumpkin reached the bottom of the hill first, for if Freddie had been first the big, heavy pumpkin would have rolled up against him with a bump, and might have hurt him. But Freddie, bumping into the pumpkin, as he did, was not hurt at all.

"Oh, you funny little boy!" cried the little girl who had laughed, as she ran up to Freddie, who was now sitting on the grass. "The pumpkin beat you in the rolling race down hill. But maybe you'll win next time."

"There isn't going to be any next time," laughed Mother Bobbsey, as she ran to pick Freddie up. "He didn't do that on purpose, little girl."

"Oh, I thought he did. Anyhow, it was funny!" and she laughed again.

"Yes, it was funny," agreed Bert. "And here comes a man after the pumpkin, I guess."

"Be careful that he doesn't take you and put you on exhibition in the tent," said Nan to her little brother.

"Will he, Mother?" asked Flossie.

"No, of course not. Nan is only joking."

"The pumpkin isn't hurt any," said Harry, helping the man lift it up on his shoulder.

"I'm glad of it," the man said. "It has won the prize, and the farmer who owns it wouldn't like it if it should be broken."

"Let's go over to the merry-go-round," suggested Freddie, who did not like so many people looking at him, for quite a crowd had gathered when word of the funny pumpkin race spread. "I want a ride on the merry-go-round."

"So do I," added Flossie.

"And then it will be time for the balloon to go up," added Bert. "Do you think the wind is too strong?" he asked his father.

"Well, it is blowing pretty hard, and it's getting worse. I think there is going to be a storm. But I see men working around the balloon, and I think they are going to send it up. Perhaps they think they can send it up and let it come down again before the storm."

"Oh, let's hurry and see it!" cried Nan, who was as much interested in the big gas bag as were the boys.

"First we'll give Flossie and Freddie a ride on the merry-go-round, I think," suggested Mrs. Bobbsey. So they all voted to have a ride, as Mr. Bobbsey wanted a chance to speak to Mr. Blipper.

But, just as had happened the other time, Mr. Blipper was not there. Bob Guess was taking tickets, and when he saw Nan he smiled.

"I'll get you the brass ring," he promised, and he did.

The children liked the lively music, and also the whirling ride on the backs of the wooden animals. Even Mrs. Bobbsey took one ride, but she said that was enough. Nan had a special ride, because Bob Guess had saved for her the brass ring, and when the other children learned that Nan was to ride for nothing, of course they wanted an extra ride, for which Mr. Bobbsey had to pay.

"When do you think Mr. Blipper will be here?" Mr. Bobbsey asked of Bob, as the party was leaving. "I want to talk to him."

"I don't know," was the boy's answer. "He doesn't stay at the merry-go-round as much as he used to. He lets me and one of his men run it. He's away a lot."

"Well, you tell him I want to see him," went on Mr. Bobbsey. "I shall be here to-morrow and the next day."

"I'll tell him," promised Bob Guess.

"Now let's go see the balloon," suggested Bert.

"They're getting ready to send it up!" exclaimed Harry, as they neared the place where the big bag, already partly filled with gas, was swaying to and fro. Over the bag was a net work of strong cords, and the cords were fastened to the rim of a large square basket. To the basket were tied ropes, and to the ends of these ropes were bags of sand, thus holding the balloon to the ground.

"What makes it go up?" asked Flossie, as she watched the swaying bag.

"Gas," explained Mr. Bobbsey. "They put in the big bag some gas, sometimes one kind and sometimes another, just like the gas in your toy balloons. This gas is so very light—it's not even so heavy as air—that it wants to go up into the air, all by itself. And when it is inside a bag the gas takes the bag up into the air with it."

"And the basket too? Doesn't it take the basket?" Freddie asked.

"Yes, the basket goes up with the balloon," said Mrs. Bobbsey.

"Who goes in the basket?" asked Freddie.

"Oh, the man," his father answered.

"Do any children go in the balloon?" called out Flossie. "Any boys or girls?"

"Oh, no!" quickly said Nan, for she did not want her little sister and brother to tease for a ride in a balloon basket.

"I'd like a ride in a balloon," murmured Freddie.

Just then the wind began to blow more strongly, and the big gas bag swayed to one side, toward a crowd of people who ran to get out of the way.

"Get more ropes!" cried one of the balloon men. "Get more ropes and sand bags!"

"That's right!" shouted another man. "There's going to be a storm. I don't know whether we ought to send the balloon up!"

"Oh, let her go!" cried several in the crowd. They did not want to be disappointed. Bert and Harry added their voices to the cries for an ascension.

"Well, we'll have to tie the balloon down until we get more gas in it," said the first man. "Come on now, more ropes and sand bags!"

While these were being brought the Bobbsey twins and their relatives drew as near to the balloon as they could get, closely looking at it. At times the big bag, partly filled with gas, swayed until it swept the ground. The basket, too, pulled and tugged at the ropes that held it down.

"What does the man do when he's in the basket?" Freddie asked.

"Oh, he sits there and rides along up in the clouds," said Bert. "I wish I could go up."

"Does he have anything to eat?" Flossie wanted to know.

"Oh, yes," said Nan. "There are things to eat in the basket. See!" And she held Flossie up so she could look over the edge and down into the basket. Of course Freddie had to be lifted up, also.

The basket seemed a cosy place. There were blankets in it, for it is often very cold high up in the air where balloons go, though it may be very warm on the earth. And there were boxes and packages containing food and many strange things at which the Bobbsey twins wondered.

The wind kept blowing harder and harder, and the crowd grew larger as word went around the fair grounds that the balloon was soon to go up.

"What about those ropes?" cried the man who was in charge of the balloon.

"They're coming," another man told him. "Be here right away!"

"Well, those lads want to hurry if this balloon isn't to go sailing off by itself! My, but the wind is blowing hard! I've a good notion to call this off. I'm afraid we're in for a bad storm."

"We can't stop it now," said the second man. "The crowd expects us to go up, and we'll have to go."

"Well, we'll try it. But we must tie the balloon down and put in more gas. It won't go up very far only half filled as it is."

Suddenly some voices cried:

"One side! One side if you please!"

It was the men coming up with ropes to tie the balloon down.

Mr. and Mrs. Bobbsey tried to gather the children close to them, to get them out of the way of the men. But, in some manner, Flossie and Freddie turned to one side, and before they knew it they were separated from their friends. And then Flossie and Freddie found themselves pushed close up against the balloon basket.

"Oh, let's get in!" cried Freddie.

"We'll just sit down for a minute and then get out," agreed Flossie.

The crowd was so excited, trying to get out of the way of the men with the coils of rope, that no one noticed what the small Bobbsey twins did. And so Freddie and Flossie climbed into the balloon basket and snuggled down in the blankets.

"Quick now with those ropes!" cried the head man. "She's going to tear loose! Feel that wind!"

There came a heavy blow, causing the balloon to sway back and forth.

"Look out!" cried another voice. "There she goes!"

Almost as he spoke there was a further scramble on the part of the crowd, and the balloon tore loose from the holding ropes before the men had time to put on the new ones.

"There she goes!" echoed the crowd. "Up goes the balloon!"

And up it went, taking Flossie and Freddie with it! Up and up it rose, shooting above the heads of the crowd.

"Oh, Freddie!" cried Flossie, "what's going to happen?"

"We're going up in a balloon!" shouted Freddie, and then he laughed. He thought it was fun.

"Oh, I want to get down!" screamed Flossie. She looked over the edge of the basket, as did her brother, and just then Mrs. Bobbsey glanced up.

"Oh, my children! Flossie and Freddie!" she gasped, pointing. "They're in the balloon!"

On the Island

There was great excitement down on the ground when the cry of Mrs. Bobbsey told her husband, the other children, and the big crowd that Flossie and Freddie had been carried away in the balloon. At first some did not believe it, and even Mr. Bobbsey found it hard to imagine that such a thing could happen.

But one look up at the swaying basket dangling from the runaway balloon showed him the faces of Flossie and Freddie looking down at the earth which seemed to be dropping away from them.

"Oh, my children! My children! Flossie! Freddie!" cried Mrs. Bobbsey, tears streaming down her cheeks, as she raised her hands toward the swiftly rising balloon.

"Get them down!"

"We'll catch 'em if they jump!"

"Get a ladder!"

"Have the man in the aeroplane go after them!"

These were some of the cries—foolish cries in some cases—that sounded on all sides as Flossie and Freddie were carried away. For how could any ladder be long enough to reach up to the balloon?

"Oh, can't we do something?" wailed Mrs. Bobbsey, holding to her husband.

"We'll save them! We'll save Flossie and Freddie," said Mr. Bobbsey. Nan was crying also, and Harry and Bert looked at each other with strange faces. They didn't know what to do or say.

Mr. Bobbsey felt the wind blowing stronger and stronger and saw the gathering storm. As he saw how fast the balloon was moving upward and onward, away from the fair grounds, he, too, was much frightened.

"How did those children get in there?" asked one of the balloon men.

"They must have crawled in the basket when we weren't looking," answered Mr. Bobbsey.

"Is there any way of saving my little children?" cried Mrs. Bobbsey.

"Now don't you worry," said the balloon man kindly. "They'll be all right if they stay in the basket. The balloon hasn't all its gas in, and it won't blow very far. It will soon come down to the ground."

"But won't they be killed?"

"No, a balloon comes down very gently when the gas gives out." said the man. "It's almost like a parachute. Your children will come down like feathers. We'll get up a searching party and go after them." He knew there was great danger but he did not want to add to Mrs. Bobbsey's fears.

"Oh, yes! Do something!" cried Mrs. Bobbsey. "We must save them!"

While down below there was all excitement and while a searching party was getting ready to start out to rescue Flossie and Freddie, the two little children themselves were safe enough in the balloon basket. That is they were safe for the time being, for they could not fall unless they climbed over the side of the basket, and they would hardly do this. They were also safe from banging into anything, for they were now high in the air, well above all trees and buildings, and there were no other balloons or any aeroplanes in sight.

At the fair grounds was an aeroplane, but it had not gone up yet, and could not, for the engine was broken, and the man had to mend it before he could make a flight. So as long as Flossie and Freddie remained in the basket they were safe.

They did not even feel the wind blow, for as they were being carried right along in the gale, being a part of it, so to speak, they did not feel it as they had when standing on the ground.

But, in spite of all this, Flossie's little heart was beating very fast and tears came into her eyes.

"Oh, Freddie!" she half sobbed, "what you s'pose's goin' to happen to us?"

"I don't know," he answered. "But anyhow we're up in a balloon and we're having a fine sail. I like a balloon, don't you, Flossie?"

Flossie thought it over for a moment. Now that the first fright was passed she rather enjoyed the quiet, easy motion. For there were no bumps as in an automobile, and there was no swaying as on the merry-go-round. It was like flying with the birds, and Flossie had always wanted to be a bird.

"It is—yes, I guess it is nice," she said. "Are we high up?"

"Not very," Freddie answered. "Don't look over the edge or you might fall out of the basket," he told his sister, as he saw her getting ready to stand on her tiptoes and peer down. Freddie had looked down once, as had Flossie, when they first felt themselves going up, and it had made him a little dizzy. He did not want Flossie to fall out.

"Let's see if we can find something to eat," suggested the little boy. "I'm hungry."

"So'm I," agreed Flossie. This was something new to think about.

They poked among the things in the balloon basket. There were funny objects, the uses of which they could only guess at, but there were also some crackers and sandwiches, as well as a bottle of milk, and some water.

"Oh, we can have a regular camp-out!" laughed Flossie. "We'll make believe we're on a steamer."

"It'll be lots of fun," agreed Freddie. So they ate and were quite happy, while those they had left behind were very much worried and miserable.

The wind blew harder and harder, but, as I have said, Flossie and Freddie did not notice it. Soon, however, they began to notice something else, and this was some drops of water.

"Oh, the balloon's leaking!" cried Flossie, as she felt a damp spot on her red cheek.

Freddie also felt some wet splashes, but he saw at once what they were.

"It's raining!" he cried. And so it was. The storm had broken.

"Raining!" cried Flossie. "And we hasn't got any umbrella!"

"We don't need one," said the little boy. "The balloon's so big it will be like an umbrella over us."

This was partly true. The bag of the balloon bulged out over the heads of the children, keeping off most of the rain. But some blew in sideways over the top of the basket, and the children would have been quite wet had they not wrapped themselves in blankets. These kept them warm and dry, for one of the blankets was of rubber.

Thus the little Bobbsey twins sailed on in a balloon, the first ride of this kind they had ever taken. Their first fright was over, but they began wondering what would happen next.

Suddenly Flossie discovered a hole in the bottom of the basket, through which she could look down to the earth. And as she looked she cried:

"Oh, Freddie, we're going down into a lake!"

Freddie looked and saw what his sister had seen. The balloon was now going down. Probably the gas had leaked out, or there may not have been more than enough to carry the balloon a short distance. At any rate it was now falling, and, as the children saw, straight toward a body of water.

"Shall we fall into the water?" asked Flossie.

"No—no, I don't guess so," Freddie answered. He hoped that was not going to happen. But as he looked down and saw the water seemingly coming nearer and nearer, though of course it was the balloon going down, the little boy did not feel at all sure but they would drop right into the lake.

"We'd better hold on hard to the basket," said Freddie, after thinking over the best thing to do. "When we get in the lake we can hold on to the basket until somebody comes."

This idea made Flossie feel a little better. She was glad she had Freddie with her, and Freddie was glad Flossie was with him.

Down, down the balloon gently dropped. The rain was pouring hard now, splashing into the lake, which was covered in some places with a blanket of fog.

Then, just when it seemed that Flossie and Freddie and the balloon would splash into the water, an island loomed in sight.

"Oh, if we could only land on the island!" cried Freddie.

And that's just what happened! Through the branches of trees the balloon crashed, this helping to stop it more gently. Down to the island it fell, the basket banging on the ground. The basket tipped over sideways, spilling Flossie and Freddie out, but not hurting them as they fell in a pile of dried leaves. Some of the things in the basket fell out with them.

Once the children were out of the balloon it rose a little, was blown along a short distance by the wind, and then, getting tangled in the tree branches, came to a stop.

"Well, we're all right now," said Freddie, as he arose and brushed the leaves from him.

"But I'm getting all wet!" sobbed Flossie. "I'm soaked!"

And so she was, as well as Freddie, for it was raining hard.

The Searching Party

Every one at the fair grounds was anxious to help Mr. and Mrs. Bobbsey get back Flossie and Freddie, who had been carried off in the runaway balloon. The men who owned the big gas bag were the first to make the right sort of plans.

"The balloon is being blown over the lake," said Mr. Trench, the owner of the big bag. "We must go in that direction."

"Over the lake!" cried Mrs. Bobbsey. "Oh, if they should fall in!"

"The balloon will float on the water," her husband told her. "The children will be all right, I'm sure."

"Yes, indeed," agreed Mr. Trench. "Don't worry, lady. We'll get your children back. The first thing to do is to go to the lake, and then we can hire a motor-boat there."

"I'm going with you!" declared Mrs. Bobbsey, as she saw the preparations being made for the searching party.

"I think you had better stay with Bert and Nan," said Mr. Bobbsey.

"Oh, we'll be all right!" Nan hastened to tell her father.

"Can't Harry and I come on the searching party?" asked Bert.

"No, I would rather not," his father answered. "You stay with your mother and Nan."

"I simply am coming with you, Dick!" said Mrs. Bobbsey, and when she spoke in that tone her husband knew there was no use trying to get her to change her mind.

"Very well," agreed Mr. Bobbsey. "We will go to the lake in my auto. Mr. Trench knows where we can hire a motor-boat."

The lake, a large one, came within a few miles of the fair grounds. The balloon man knew in which direction the water lay, and he had seen the wind carrying the big gas bag toward the water.

"Bert, you and Nan and Harry must go back to Meadow Brook Farm," directed Mr. Bobbsey. "I'll see if I can't hire an auto to take you there, as it is going to storm soon. It's sprinkling now."

"We'll take them back," offered a gentleman who had come to the fair with his wife in their auto. "I know where Meadow Brook Farm is. We'll take these children there."

"Thank you, very much," said Mr. Bobbsey. "And tell your uncle and aunt what has happened, Bert. Tell them we expect to be home before night with Flossie and Freddie."

"Oh, if we only can be!" exclaimed Mrs. Bobbsey.

"We'll find the little ones all right—never fear!" said Mr. Trench. "If you're ready now, we'll start."

So while Nan, Bert and Harry remained behind in charge of Mr. Blackford, who had offered to take them home in his automobile, Mr. and Mrs. Bobbsey, with some men who had charge of the balloon, started off to go to the lake, there to hire a boat and search for Flossie and Freddie.

"They're out of sight. How far away they must be!" sighed Mrs. Bobbsey, as she entered the automobile. She looked up, but could not see the balloon, so fast had it been blown away.

"They aren't so far as it seems," declared Mr. Trench. "It's getting foggy, and it's going to rain hard soon."

As Bert, Nan, and Harry were getting in Mr. Blackford's automobile to go to Meadow Brook Farm, Bob Guess came hurrying up through the rain. The merry-go-round, as well as other amusements at the fair, had shut down on account of the storm.

"Where's your father?" asked Bob of Bert. "I've something to tell him. Where is he?"

"He's gone off after the balloon. Flossie and Freddie are in it," Nan answered.

"Whew! Those little children taking a balloon ride!" cried Bob. "How did they dare?"

"It was an accident," Harry explained. "They didn't mean to."

"Well, tell your father I want to see him when he gets back," said Bob, as he hurried back to the merry-go-round. "I have something to tell him about Mr. Blipper."

However, Bert and Nan had other things to think about then than about Mr. Blipper. They were worried over what might happen to Flossie and Freddie.

Meanwhile, Mr. and Mrs. Bobbsey were hastening toward the lake. Mr. Bobbsey drove his car as fast as he dared through the storm. It was now raining hard.

"How long would the balloon stay up in the air?" asked Mr. Bobbsey of Mr. Trench.

"It all depends. On a hot day, when the sun warms the gas, it would stay up a long time. But when it is cool, like this, and rains, it will not stay up so long. It will come down gently, and I am sure the children will not be hurt."

As they drove along they stopped now and then to ask people if they had seen the runaway balloon. Many had, and all said it was sailing toward the lake.

When the lake was reached and a motor-boat had been found which would take them out on the water, several men said they had seen the big gas bag beginning to go down near Hemlock Island, the largest island in the lake.

"If they have only landed there they may be all right," Mrs. Bobbsey said. "Oh, hurry and get there, Dick!"

"We'll hurry all we can," her husband told her, as they got into the boat to continue the search. "But this is a bad storm. We must be careful."

On the Rocks

The whole world seemed a very dreary and unhappy place to Mr. and Mrs. Bobbsey as they started off in the motor-boat to look for Flossie and Freddie. In the first place, if one of the little Bobbsey twins had just been lost—plain lost—as Flossie was in the cornfield, it would have been sad enough. But when both tots were missing, and when the last seen of them had been a sight of them shooting away in a balloon through a gathering storm, well, it was enough to make any father and mother feel very unhappy.

Besides this, there was the rain, and as the motor-boat, in charge of Captain Craig, swung out into the lake, the big, pelting drops came down harder than ever.

"Oh, what a sad, sad day!" sighed Mrs. Bobbsey. "And it started off so happily, too!"

"Perhaps it will end happily," said Mr. Bobbsey, hopefully. "It will not be night for several hours yet, and before then we may find Flossie and Freddie. In fact I'm sure we shall!"

"I think so, too," declared Mr. Trench, the owner of the balloon. "That craft of mine wasn't filled with enough gas to go far, and it had to come down soon."

"But where would it come down? That's the point!" cried Mrs. Bobbsey. "If it came down in the lake—"

"It's on Hemlock Island, take my word for it!" growled out Captain Craig, in whose motor-boat the searching party was riding. It was not because he was cross that his voice had a growling sound. It was just naturally hoarse. He was out on the water so much, often in the cold and rain, that he seemed to have an everlasting cold. "We'll find the balloon and the children, too, on Hemlock Island," he went on. "Half a dozen men I talked to, just before you came, said they saw something big and black, like an airship, swooping down on the island. We'll find 'em there, never fear!"

"How far are we from Hemlock Island?" asked Mr. Bobbsey of Captain Craig, when they had been in the motor-boat about fifteen minutes.

"Oh, a few miles—just a few miles," was the answer.

"And how long will it take to get there?" Mrs. Bobbsey asked.

"Well, that's hard to say," was the answer. "It might take us a long while, and again it might not take us so long."

"Why is that?" asked Mr. Bobbsey, wondering whether Bert and Nan would be all right, left to themselves as they were. But then they would have their uncle, aunt, and cousin to look after them.

"Well," went on Captain Craig, as he steered the boat to one side, "you see it's getting thicker and thicker—I mean the weather. The rain is coming down harder and it's getting foggy, too. I can't very well see where to steer, and I have to run at slow speed. So it will take me longer to get to Hemlock Island than if it was a clear day and I could run as fast as my boat would go."

"Well, get there as soon as you can," begged Mrs. Bobbsey. "I'm sure if Flossie and Freddie are on the island in all this rain they will be terribly frightened!"

"Well, they may be—a little," admitted Mr. Bobbsey. "But Flossie and Freddie are brave children. They'll make the best of things I'm sure!"

The motor-boat went chug-chugging its way across the big lake, not running as fast as it could have done on a fair day. The rain poured down, making a hissing sound in the water. Those in the boat wore rubber coats, for Captain Craig had supplied them at his boathouse before starting out. He owned a boat dock, and also a fishing pier, and supplied pleasure parties with nearly everything they needed for fair weather or stormy.

Suddenly Mrs. Bobbsey, who was straining her eyes to peer through the mist and rain, uttered a cry.

"There's something!" she called out.

"Where?" asked her husband, and Captain Craig leaned forward, his hands gripping the spokes of the steering wheel.

"Right straight ahead," went on Mrs. Bobbsey. "Something black is looming up in the fog. Maybe it's the balloon!"

"We can't be anywhere near the island yet," said the captain. "That is unless I'm away off my course. But we'll soon find out what it is."

They could all see the black object now, though it looked dim and uncertain, for a fog was settling down over the lake and the mist and vapor, together with the rain, made it hard to see more than a few feet ahead.

"It's a boat!" suddenly cried Mr. Bobbsey. "A large boat."

And that is what it was.

"Ahoy there!" called Captain Craig in his deep voice. "Ahoy there!"

"Ahoy!" answered the men in the boat.

"Have you seen anything of a runaway balloon?" asked Mr. Trench. "Mine got away from the Bolton County Fair, and it had two little children in the balloon basket. Have you seen them?"

Mr. and Mrs. Bobbsey and all in the motor boat waited anxiously for the answer. Captain Craig had shut off his engine so its noise would not drown the words of those in the other boat.

"We saw something big and black sailing through the air over our heads about an hour ago," was the answer. "We thought it was the aeroplane from the fair grounds."

"That was my balloon!" declared Mr. Trench.

"Did you see anything of my children?" Mrs. Bobbsey begged to know.

"No. But we couldn't see very well on account of the fog and because the balloon—if that's what it was—kept up pretty high," came the answer.

"Which way was she heading?" Captain Craig wanted to know, this being his sailor way of asking which way the balloon was going.

"Due north," answered one of the men in the other boat, which was a craft containing a number of fishermen.

"Towards Hemlock Island," stated another.

"Well, we're going in the right direction," went on Captain Craig. "Much obliged," he called to the fishermen, as the motor-boat again started off through the fog.

Soon the vessel that had been hailed was lost to sight in the mist, and again all eyes, including those of Mr. and Mrs. Bobbsey, were strained in looking for a first sight of Hemlock Island.

"Are you warm enough?" asked Mr. Bobbsey of his wife, wrapping the rubber coat more closely about her.

"Oh, yes. I'm not thinking of myself," she answered, with a sigh. "I am worried about my darlings!"

"I think they'll come out of it all right," said her husband. "Flossie and Freddie, as well as Bert and Nan, have been in many a scrape, but the Bobbsey luck seems to hold good. They always get out all right."

"Yes. And I hope they will this time," answered Mrs. Bobbsey, trying to appear more cheerful.

For a while they ran along in silence, every one peering out into the rain and the mist striving to catch sight, if not of the balloon, at least of the shore of Hemlock Island.

"My, but this fog is getting thicker and thicker!" exclaimed Captain Craig. "I'll have to go a bit slower yet."

He cut down the speed of the engine until the boat was moving at less than half speed. But even this did not save her from an accident which came a short time later.

Suddenly, as they were cruising along, every eye on the lookout for a sight of the island, there came a violent crash. All in the boat were thrown forward.

"Gracious!" exclaimed Mrs. Bobbsey, as she struggled to regain her seat.

"What have we struck?" Mr. Bobbsey asked.

"We've struck Hemlock Island," said Captain Craig grimly. "We've fairly bumped into it. I ought to have known I was somewhere near it. We've fairly rammed it, and we're on the rocks!"

"'On the rocks!'" repeated Mrs. Bobbsey. "Are we in danger?"

"That's what I'm going to find out," said the captain. "At least we can't sink, for we're right on shore," and as he spoke the fog blew away for a moment, showing a bleak shore of rocks with hemlock trees a little way up from the beach. "Yes, sir, we ran plumb on the rocks!" muttered Captain Craig, as he stood up and tried to peer through the fog that was now closing in again.

Two Little Sailors

Now it is time for us to inquire what was happening to Freddie and Flossie, the two smaller Bobbsey twins. They had fallen out of the balloon basket when the big gas bag was blown down on Hemlock Island in the storm. But Flossie and Freddie had toppled out on piles of soft, dried leaves, so they were not hurt. But, as Flossie had said, she was soaking wet.

"We ought to have umbrellas," said Freddie, as he felt the drops of rain pelting down. "If we had umbrellas this would be fun, 'cause we aren't hurt from our balloon ride."

"No, we aren't hurt," agreed Flossie, "'ceptin' I'm jiggled up a lot."

"So'm I," Freddie stated. "I'm jiggled, too!"

"And we hasn't got any umbrella, and I'm gettin' wetter'n wetter!" half sobbed Flossie.

Indeed it was raining harder, and as the fog was closing in on the children they could not see very far on any side of them.

It was not the first time the small Bobbsey twins had been lost together, nor the first time they had been in trouble. And, as he had done more than once, Freddie began to think of some way by which he could comfort Flossie.

The little boy was hungry, and he felt that if he could get something to eat it would make him feel better. And surely what made him feel better ought to make Flossie happier if she had some of the same.

"Are you hungry, Flossie?" he asked.

"Yes, I am," answered the little girl.

"Well, let's eat some more of the things that were in the balloon basket," proposed her brother. "They tumbled out when we did. I can see some of 'em mixed up with the blankets and other things."

When the bumping of the balloon basket had spilled out Flossie and Freddie it had also toppled out the supply of food and the tools and instruments the balloon men had intended using on their sail through the air.

"Let's get 'em before the rain soaks 'em all up," suggested Flossie, for the rain was now pouring down on everything.

"I guess that balloon won't be any good any more," said Freddie, as he looked at the big gas bag, now almost empty and tangled in the trees and bushes.

"No, I guess we won't ever get another ride in it," agreed Flossie.

That part was true enough; but, later, the balloon men took the bag from the island, mended the holes in it, and went up in many a flight from other fair grounds.

Gathering up some of the spilled food gave Flossie and Freddie something to do, and, for a time, they forgot about the rain pouring down. But it was the kind of rain one could not easily forget for very long, and after putting some tin boxes of crackers under an overhanging stump, to keep the food dry, and after eating some, Flossie exclaimed:

"Oh, I don't like it to be so wet!" Then she wept a little.

Freddie did not like it, either, but he made up his mind he must be brave and not cry. Not that Flossie could not be brave, too, but she didn't just then happen to think of it.

"I know what we can do!" Freddie exclaimed. "We can wrap the rubber blanket around us, and that will be like an umbrella—almost!"

"Oh, yes!" cried Flossie! "That will keep us from getting wet!"

And the rubber blanket turned out to be a fairly good umbrella. It was large enough for Flossie and Freddie to put over their shoulders and walk under. And it was while they were thus walking through the woods, wondering what would happen next and if their father and mother would ever find them, that Freddie saw something.

"Oh, Flossie! There's a house!" he shouted.

"Where?" demanded the little girl.

"Right over there! Among the trees! Down near the shore!"

Freddie pointed and Flossie, looking, saw dimly through the fog the outlines of some sort of building.

"Let's go there and they can telephone to daddy that we're here," said Flossie. "I guess we're all right now. And maybe Bert and Nan will wish they'd come on a balloon ride with us."

"Maybe," agreed Freddie, as he tramped along with his sister under the rubber blanket toward the building on the shore of the lake.

But alas for the hopes of the children! When they reached the place they found that what Freddie had thought was a house was only an old empty cabin. It had once been used by campers or by fishermen, and at one time may have been a cosy place. But now the glass in the windows was broken, the door hung sagging by one hinge, and inside there was a rusty stove which showed no signs of a warm, cheerful fire.

"There's nobody here," said Flossie sadly, after they had looked inside and had seen that the shack was deserted.

"Well, but it doesn't rain so hard inside as it does outside," remarked Freddie. "Let's go in. This blanket makes me tired."

The rubber covering was rather heavy for the little children, and they were glad to step inside the cabin. Even though the roof leaked in places, there were spots where it did not. Picking out one of these spaces, Freddie moved some boxes over to it, and he and his sister sat down, tired and wet, but feeling better now that they were within some sort of shelter.

"This isn't a very nice place," Flossie observed, looking around.

"No. But it's better'n being outside," stated Freddie. "And maybe there's a bed in the next room." The cabin consisted of two rooms, the door between them being shut. "I'm going to look," Freddie went on.

"No, don't!" begged Flossie, clutching Freddie by the sleeve.

"Why not?" he asked. "Don't you want me to look in that room and see if there's a bed? 'Cause maybe we'll have to stay all night."

"Don't look!" begged Flossie "Maybe—maybe Mr. Blipper is in there!"

"Mr. Blipper?" echoed Freddie. "What would he be doing here? He's at his merry-go-round."

"No, he isn't at his merry-go-round," insisted Flossie. "'Cause we was there and he wasn't there when daddy wanted to ask him about the coat and the lap robe. Maybe Mr. Blipper's in that room, and I don't like him—he's so cross!"

"Yes, he's cross," agreed Freddie. "And he was mean to Bob Guess. But maybe Mr. Blipper isn't in that room. I'm going to look!"

But Freddie never did. He got down off the old box he was using for a seat, under a part of the roof that didn't leak, when Flossie gave a cry, and pointed out-of-doors.

"Look!" she exclaimed.

"Is somebody coming?" Freddie wanted to know.

"No, but I see a boat," Flossie went on. "We can get in the boat and row back on the fair grounds and we'll be all right."

Freddie looked to where she pointed and saw a rowboat drawn up on the shore.

"If it's got oars in we could row," he said, for both he and his little sister knew something of handling boats, their father having taught them.

"Let's go down and look," proposed Flossie. "It isn't raining so hard now."

The big drops were not, indeed, pelting down quite so fast, but it was still far from dry.

Getting under the rubber blanket again, the children ran out of the cabin and toward the boat. They were delighted to find oars in it, and, seeing that the rowboat was in good shape, Freddie got in.

"Ouch!" he exclaimed as he sat down on a wet seat. "Here, wait a minute before you sit there, Flossie. I'll put the rubber blanket down to sit on."

The inside of the rubber blanket was dry, and Freddie put the wet side down on the wooden seat. This gave the children something more comfortable to sit on than a wet piece of wood.

"We'll each take an oar and row," proposed Freddie, for he and Flossie were sitting on the same seat. This was the only way to use the same rubber blanket.

Loosening the rope by which the boat was made fast to a stump on shore, Freddie pushed out into the lake. The rain had almost stopped now, and the children were feeling happier.

"Now we'll row home," announced Freddie.

"Had we better go back and get some of the crackers we left under the stump?" asked Flossie. "Maybe it's a long way to the fair grounds or to Meadow Brook Farm, and we might get hungry."

"Oh, I guess we'll soon be home," said Freddie, hopefully. "Come on and row, Flossie."

Together they rowed the boat out from shore. But they could not make the heavy craft go very fast. There was water in the bottom, probably from the rain and perhaps because the boat leaked. But Freddie and Flossie did not think about this, even though their feet were getting wet. Or, at least, wetter. Their feet were already wet from having tramped about in the heavy rain.

"We'll soon be home now," said Freddie again.

They were some little distance out from the shore, two brave but tired and miserable little sailors, when, all at once, it began to rain again.

"Oh, dear!" cried Flossie, letting go her oar, "I'm getting all soaked again!"

"Don't you care," advised her brother. "Keep on rowing!"

But Flossie cried, shook her head, and would not pick up the oar. Freddie could not row the boat alone, and he did not know what to do. Down pelted the rain, harder than before.

"I want to go back where we were!" sobbed Flossie. "Back to the cabin. Maybe we can build a fire in the stove and get warm! I'm cold!"

"All right; we'll go back!" agreed Freddie. He was beginning to fear it was not so easy to row home as he had hoped.

Down came the rain, and with it came a fog. Soon the children were enveloped in the white mist, and they could see only a little distance from the boat in which they sat.

"Come on! Row!" called Freddie to his sister. "We'll row back to the cabin."

"How do you know where it is?" Flossie asked, as she took up the oar again.

"Oh, I guess I can find it," said her brother. "You hold your oar still in the water and I'll pull on mine and turn us around." He knew how to do this quite well, and soon the boat was turned, and the children were again pulling as hard as they could pull.

It was by good luck and not by any skill of theirs that they soon reached land again. They might, for all they knew about it, have rowed out into the middle of the lake.

But soon a bumping sound told them they had reached shore, and Freddie scrambled out and held the boat while Flossie made her way to land.

"Is it the same place?" she asked, as Freddie reached for the rubber blanket.

"Yes, I can see the old cabin. We'll go up there and get warm."

Up the little hill, through the rain, trudged the children, getting what shelter they could under the blanket. Even Freddie was beginning to lose heart now, for he could see that darkness was coming on, and they were far from home. The rain, too, was pouring down harder than ever.

"Oh, dear! Oh, dear!" sighed Flossie.

"Don't cry!" begged her brother. "I'll make a fire and we'll eat some more crackers. I'll go get them from under the stump."

"I'll go with you," declared Flossie, firmly, "I'm not going to stay alone."

Together they pulled out some of the lunch they had found in the balloon basket. Back to the shack they went, and Freddie was looking about for some matches in the old cabin when Flossie suddenly called out:

"Hark! I hear something!"

A Happy Meeting

Mr. and Mrs. Bobbsey and the friends who had gone with them in Captain Craig's motor-boat to search for the runaway balloon, waited anxiously after they had run on the rocks for what was to happen next.

"Is there any danger?" asked Mrs. Bobbsey.

"No, lady, there doesn't seem to be—that is, if you mean danger of sinking," said Captain Craig. "As I remarked at first, we're plumb fast on the rocks. But maybe if we were to get out and thus lighten the boat, she would float off the rocks and we could keep on."

"That's a good idea!" declared Mr. Bobbsey. "We must keep on, no matter what happens, and find those children!"

"I think we'll find them!" declared Mr. Trench, and he seemed so much in earnest that Mrs. Bobbsey asked:

"When?"

"Very soon now," answered the balloon man. "If my gas bag came down here on Hemlock Island—that's where we are now—it won't take long to search all over it and find your Flossie and Freddie. That's what I think."

"But first let me see how badly the boat is damaged," went on the captain. "I'm afraid it's in bad shape."

"Can't we get away from here?" asked Mrs. Bobbsey. "That is, I mean, after we find the children? I wouldn't go until we have found them!" she exclaimed.

"It all depends on what shape my boat is in," went on the captain. "As soon as you are all out I'll take a look."

The searching party stood about in the rain on the shore of Hemlock Island under the dripping trees, the drops splashing on their rubber coats, while Captain Craig looked over his boat. He took some little time to do this, and at last he shook his head in gloomy fashion.

"Well?" asked Mr. Bobbsey.

"Not well—bad!" answered the captain. "We can't go on until the boat is mended. She isn't as badly smashed as I thought, and it doesn't leak much, which is a good thing. But I can't use the engine to drive her along until it's fixed. We'll have to stay on the island until I get help, I guess."

"How are we going to get help in all this rain and fog?" Mr. Bobbsey wanted to know.

"There used to be some campers' huts here," said the captain. "Maybe some of those fellows left a rowboat. I could go over to the mainland in that and get help. Some of you can come with me if you like."

"I'm not going to!" announced Mrs. Bobbsey. "I'm going to stay here and find Flossie and Freddie!"

"So am I, my dear!" added Mr. Bobbsey.

"Well, then, let's look around for a boat. If I find one I'll go for help in it, and you can stay here," said Captain Craig.

He made his own damaged craft fast close to the shore, and then the searching party set off through the woods to look for a cabin, a rowboat, and for the missing children.

"It ought to be easy to see that balloon, it's so big," said Captain Craig.

"I can spot that balloon of mine as soon as any one, I guess," said Mr. Trench. "This isn't the first time I've hunted for it. You never can tell exactly where a balloon will come down."

Through the underbrush, between trees, and in the dripping rain and swirling fog, the searching party tramped on. Suddenly one of the men gave a cry.

"I see something!" he shouted.

"Is it my children?" Mrs. Bobbsey asked, her voice trembling with eagerness.

"No, I think it's the balloon," was the answer.

And the balloon it was. Draped over bushes and trees was the big gas bag, now almost emptied of the vapor that had lifted it and carried it away from the fair grounds with Flossie and Freddie in the basket.

"Oh, but where are my little ones—my Bobbsey twins?" cried the mother.

"They must be somewhere around here," said Captain Craig.

And then, thrilling the hearts of all, came two young voices, calling:

"Daddy! Mother! Here we are! Oh, we're so glad you came! Here we are!"

Out of the woods rushed Flossie and Freddie, to be caught up in the arms of Mother and Daddy Bobbsey.

"We—we were in the hut!" breathlessly explained Flossie. "And I heard a noise, and I said for Freddie to hark, and he harked, and then we heard talking and we ran out and—and here we are!"

"Yes, darlings, here you are!" cried Mrs. Bobbsey, tears running down her cheeks. "But, oh, why did you ever do it? Why did you get into the balloon?"

"Oh, jest 'cause," answered Freddie. And they all laughed at his answer.

Bert, Nan, and Bob

While this happy meeting and reunion was taking place on Hemlock Island and while the smaller Bobbsey twins were thus made happy by finding their father and mother again, Bert and Nan were very unhappy back at Meadow Brook Farm. They had safely reached the home of their uncle and aunt, being taken there in Mr. Blackford's automobile.

"Oh, dear me, what dreadful news!" exclaimed Aunt Sarah, when told about Flossie and Freddie having been carried away in the balloon. "Shall we ever see those dear children again?"

"Of course we shall, Mother!" said Uncle Daniel, with a laugh. "Don't worry, Flossie and Freddie will be all right."

And of course Flossie and Freddie were, in the end, only Bert and Nan and their uncle, aunt, and cousin did not know that then, so of course they worried.

The storm which had been only threatening when Bert and his sister had been sent home from the fair grounds now broke, and it rained hard. At Meadow Brook, as on most farms, little could be done when it rained, and the children saw Uncle Daniel and Aunt Sarah sitting around talking in low tones.

"I just wish I could do something!" gloomily remarked Bert, as he stood with his face pressed against the window, down which the rain drops were chasing each other.

"So do I," echoed Nan. "I think they might have let us help them look for Flossie and Freddie."

"I guess your father and mother knew best," said Harry. "And I think the balloon will come down soon in all this rain. It sure is pouring!"

And it was. The storm kept up all day, and in the afternoon, when Nan was on the verge of tears and Bert had almost made up his mind to go back alone to the fair grounds and see if he could hear any news, there came a knock at the back door.

"There's some one!" cried Nan, jumping from her chair.

"Maybe it's Flossie and Freddie come back!" added Bert.

"They wouldn't knock at the back door," observed his aunt. "Harry, go and see who it is. Maybe it's good news."

Harry returned in a few moments to say:

"It's that boy from the merry-go-round, Bob Guess. He wants to see your father, Bert."

"Well, dad isn't here, and—"

"I told him, and then he said he wants to see some of us—my father I think he means. He has something to tell."

"Bring him in here," advised Uncle Daniel, who was trying to read the paper, though half the time he had it upside down, for he was thinking too much about poor Flossie and Freddie to pay attention to anything else.

Bob Guess came in, dripping wet, though not as ragged as when Bert and Nan had first seen him.

"What's the matter?" asked Uncle Daniel in his jolly voice. "Can't you do any business at the fair on account of the rain?"

"No. And I don't want ever to do any more business at the fair," answered Bob, in such strange tones that they all looked at him.

"Don't you like the merry-go-round any more?" Bert asked.

"Oh, it isn't that," said Bob. "It's that man Blipper. I can't stand him any longer! He blamed me for poor business to-day, and it wasn't my fault at all. In the first place, all the people went over to see the balloon go up. Hardly anybody took rides on our machine. Then the children—I mean your little brother and sister," he said to Nan, "got carried off, and everybody got scared for fear something would happen to their children, and they wouldn't even let 'em ride on the merry-go-round. And then the rain came down, and Blipper seemed to blame me for that."

"He isn't a very fair sort of man, even if he has his machine at a county fair," joked Uncle Daniel.

"He's terribly ugly," blurted out Bob Guess. "And I think he's worse than that!"

"What do you mean?" asked Bert.

"Well, I think he takes things that don't belong to him," went on Bob. "Your father lost a coat some time ago, didn't he?" the strange boy asked the older Bobbsey twins.

"Yes, at our Sunday school picnic," answered Nan.

"And a lap robe was taken from our auto about the same time," added Bert.

"That's what I thought," said Bob. "Well, would you know any of your father's papers if you saw them?" he asked, as he began to fumble in his pocket. "I mean would you know his writing on a letter, or something like that?"

"Of course I know my father's writing!" declared Bert.

"Well, look at this!" said Bob Guess suddenly. He held out an envelope, torn open at one end as if the letter had been taken out.

"That's father's writing!" exclaimed Bert. "This is a letter he wrote to Mr. Clarkson who buys lumber from dad. I know, for I've been in the office when he called. I guess my father must have been in a hurry and he addressed this letter himself with a pen, and didn't wait for his typewriter to do it. That's my father's writing!"

"Well," said Bob slowly, "I found that letter in the tent where Mr. Blipper and I live. We sort of camp out at the different fair grounds where we set up the merry-go-round," he added. "I have to live with Mr. Blipper. He claims I'm his adopted son, but I don't like him for an adopted father. Anyhow, I saw this letter drop out of his coat. He didn't see it, and I picked it up."

"Was it my father's coat?" asked Nan.

"That I don't know," Bob answered. "I never saw your father wearing his coat. But Mr. Blipper used to have an old ragged coat, and right after we had that breakdown at the Sunday school picnic grounds he had a new coat.

"I asked him where he got it, 'cause I thought maybe he'd get me one, I was so ragged, and he said it wasn't any of my affair where he got his coats. Then the next day I noticed he had a new robe as a blanket for his bed. I asked him about that, too, 'cause I had only a ragged quilt, and he told me to keep still.

"So when you folks asked me if I had seen your father's coat and the lap robe I didn't know for sure, and, anyhow, I was afraid to say anything. But I'm not afraid any more."

"Why not?" asked Uncle Daniel.

"'Cause," answered Bob, "I heard Mr. Blipper and his partner, a man named Hardy, quarreling to-day. First it started over bad business on account of the rain and nobody riding on the merry-go-round because the balloon was going up. Then I heard my name mentioned and the quarrel grew worse. Mr. Hardy said Mr. Blipper didn't have any right to treat me as mean as he does.

Mr. Blipper said he'd do as he pleased, and then Mr. Hardy said if he did he'd tell on Mr. Blipper."

"What did he mean—tell on him?" asked Bert.

"I don't know, exactly," answered Bob Guess. "It was all sort of queer. Maybe Mr. Hardy meant he was going to tell about Mr. Blipper taking your father's coat and the lap robe."

"I'm sure Mr. Blipper must have daddy's coat," declared Nan. "This letter dropped from the pocket, and there was money and there were other papers, too."

"I don't know anything about them," murmured Bob.

"Well, I know something!" cried Bert. "And that is this! What Mr. Hardy said he was going to tell on Blipper about was you, Bob Guess!"

"Me?" cried the strange boy.

"Yes, you! I don't believe you belong to Mr. Blipper at all!"

Joyous Times

Bob Guess could, for a moment, only stare at Bert after this strange remark.

"What do you mean?" asked the boy from the merry-go-round. "Don't I have to stay with Mr. Blipper if I don't want to?"

"I don't believe you do," went on Bert. "I heard my father and mother talking about it," he explained to the others. "My father said he was going to find out if Mr. Blipper had really adopted you. And if you stay here until my father comes back he'll have this Mr. Blipper arrested for taking his coat. Just you stay here, Bob!"

"I'd like to," sighed the unhappy lad. "I don't like Blipper. And if I go back now, after having run away again, he'll beat me!"

"We won't let him!" exclaimed Aunt Sarah. "Here, I'll get you some dry clothes. Harry has a suit you can wear. And then we'll see about this Blipper man!"

As she started to leave the room to get some dry clothing for Bob Guess, who was soaking wet, there was a noise and some excitement out in the yard. Then Nan caught the sound of a voice she well knew.

"Oh, it's Flossie!" she cried. "It's Flossie! They've found them!"

Instantly there was a mad rush for the door, and a little later into the warm, comfortable farmhouse came Mr. and Mrs. Bobbsey with the missing twins—poor little wet twins, but happy for all that.

"Oh, hurray!" cried Bert, grabbing hold of Harry and dancing around the room with him. "Now everything's all right!"

"Oh, what happened to you?" asked Nan through her tears, as she kissed first Freddie and then Flossie and then both the twins at the same time.

"Well, we found them!" said Mr. Bobbsey to Uncle Daniel.

"Where?"

"On Hemlock Island, where the balloon came down. The motor-boat we got to go across the lake was also wrecked on the same island. And Flossie and Freddie started out in a rowboat to come to shore, but they got lost in the fog and had to turn back. And they heard us on the island and came to us."

"How did you get off if your motor-boat was wrecked?" asked Bert.

"Oh, Captain Craig managed to patch it up, and it got us back to the mainland. We went back to where we had started from—Captain Craig's dock—and then we came on here in my auto. Oh, what a day this has been!" exclaimed Mr. Bobbsey, sinking wearily into a chair.

"But it all ends happily," said his wife. "Oh, here's Bob Guess!" she exclaimed, as she noticed the strange boy.

"Yes, and he knows where your missing coat is, and the lap robe, too!" exclaimed Bert. "Blipper has 'em!"

"My, everything is happening at once!" laughed Mother Bobbsey. "But we must get Flossie and Freddie to bed. They have had a hard day!"

"Don't want to go to bed!" declared Freddie. "Want to see Bob. Did you bring the merry-go-round?" he asked.

"As if he hadn't troubles enough!" exclaimed Nan.

Finally the smaller Bobbsey twins were induced to take off their damp clothes and go to bed, where they fell asleep almost as soon as their heads touched the pillows. They were very weary, for they had had an exciting trip, though they did not really think so at the time.

When all the stories had been told of how the children had been found on the island, how the motor-boat had been repaired, and of the trip back to the mainland safely made, Mr. Bobbsey turned to Bob Guess.

"Now we can give you a little attention," he said. "What's your trouble?"

So Bob told the same story he had related to Bert and Nan.

"I always thought there was something wrong about Blipper!" declared the father of the Bobbsey twins. "Now I know it! We'll get after Blipper in the morning. You stay here to-night, Bob. We'll call you Bob Guess for the present, but I think we can find a better name for you soon. I think we shall all feel better for a little rest."

"And something to eat," added Aunt Sarah. "I'm sure you must be starved!"

"I am!" admitted Mother Bobbsey. "I couldn't eat when I was worrying about Flossie and Freddie, but now that they are safe I could eat two meals at once!"

There was a merry party around the farmhouse supper table, while the little Bobbsey twins slept peacefully upstairs, probably dreaming about their trip in the balloon.

The storm was over the next day, and after talking to several newspaper reporters who came to Meadow Brook Farm to get the story of the wonderful trip of Flossie and Freddie, Daddy Bobbsey started for the fair grounds with Bert and Bob Guess. They stopped in the village to get a policeman and also a lawyer.

"If Blipper wants to put up a fight we'll be ready for him," said Mr. Bobbsey.

But when the fair grounds were reached there was no Blipper to be found. In the night he had packed up his merry-go-round and had traveled on, leaving no word as to where he was going.

"I don't care where he's gone!" said the partner, Mr. Hardy. "I'm through with him. We've broken up the partnership. I sold my share to him. I don't care to have anything to do with such a man. He's a thief!"

"Perhaps you can tell us about this boy—Bob Guess," suggested Mr. Bobbsey.

"Yes, I can. I told Blipper I'd tell, after I found out he'd taken a coat and a robe that didn't belong to him. He carted them away with him too, so if they're yours there's no use looking for them," he added to Mr. Bobbsey.

"Oh, well, I gave them up for lost some time ago," said the lumber dealer. "I managed to get copies of the papers that were in my pockets, and I wouldn't wear the coat again, anyhow. But what about Bob?"

Then Mr. Hardy told the story. Mr. Blipper had found Bob, a little chap, wandering about the streets of a big city. The boy, it seemed, lived with an Italian who said he had once known Bob's father and mother who had been dead some time.

"I don't know how Blipper managed it, but he got the boy away from the Italian," said Mr. Hardy, "and gave out that he had adopted Bob Guess as his son. But I knew better, though I didn't see much use in telling about it. In fact, I didn't know who to tell. I didn't know who would look after Bob if Blipper didn't, in his own rough way. So I kept still, though after Blipper and I quarreled, I threatened to tell. And now I have."

"I'll see if we can find Bob's relatives," said Mr. Bobbsey. "If we can't, why, I think he will be provided for."

"Oh, I'm so glad!" exclaimed Bob. "I'd rather belong to anybody but Blipper!"

And, a few days later, inquiries having been made, it was found that Bob's father and mother had died in a distant city and that, there being no one to look after the poor boy, the Italian had taken him in. Then, in some manner, Blipper got him and treated him harshly.

Bob was only a small boy when Mr. Blipper got control of him, and the merry-go-round man told a wrong story about having taken the lad from an orphan asylum. If Bob had been in an asylum he would have been well treated, and no person would have been allowed to take him away until they had been looked up, to make sure the boy would be well cared for.

Mr. Blipper forged, or made out himself, the papers showing that Bob was his adopted son, and Bob was too small to know any better when Mr. Blipper told him this and also told how he had been taken from an asylum. Bob had only a dim remembrance of the Italian who looked after him for a time, following the death of the boy's father and mother. The Italian was much kinder than Mr. Blipper had been.

"How would you like to come and live on this farm with me?" asked Uncle Daniel, when it became evident that Bob had no folks living.

"Do you mean forever?" asked the boy, delight showing in his eyes.

"Yes, forever. Come here as my son. I'll adopt you properly. Harry always wanted a brother, and now he can have one. Will you come?"

"Will I come?" cried Bob. "I'll come—*twice!*" he laughed.

"Then it's settled," said Uncle Daniel. "And from now on your name will be Bob Bobbsey!"

And so it was.

"And daddy never found his coat after all!" said Nan, when, several days later, they were talking over the wonderful things that had happened.

"No, but I found a brother!" laughed Harry, who was very happy to have Bob live with him.

The whole adventure had been a lot of fun, but more good times awaited them which will be related in "The Bobbsey Twins Camping Out."

And then came happy days and joyous times for all. Though Blipper's merry-go-round had been taken away from the fair grounds, there were enough other amusements.

Mr. Trench even got his balloon back, had it mended, and the regular man went up in it several times to the great delight of the crowds. But you may be sure Mrs. Bobbsey watched Flossie and Freddie very closely, to see that they did not get near the big basket. The little brother and sister were objects of curiosity wherever they went on the fair grounds, for the newspapers had published stories of their strange trip, all alone, in a balloon to Hemlock Island.

"When I grow up," declared Freddie, "I'm going to run an airship."

"Well, I'm never going to run a merry-go-round; I've had enough of them!" declared Bob Guess—or, to give him the name he was to have from then on, Bob Bobbsey.

"Well, we certainly had plenty of adventures at the Bolton County Fair," remarked Bert, when the exhibition came to a close.

"Yes, indeed!" cried all of the others.

And here let us say good-by.

THE END

CPSIA information can be obtained at www.ICGtesting.com
Printed in the USA
BVOW031846130612

292594BV00002B/39/P